MW00884725

Copyright © 2015 by Jaid Black.

Republished March 2017.

Publisher: Valentina Antonia, LLC.

No Way Out: Kari is the 8th book and 11th installment of an ongoing serial. For maximum enjoyment, it is recommended the serial be read in order:

No Way Out: Kari

Trek Mi Q'an: Book 8

By Jaid Black

Dedication

This book is dedicated to all my loyal fans who have waited so im/patiently for Kari's story. Thank you for not giving up on me.

Prologue

Three Moon-risings Outside Khan-Gori Airspace

Zyrus Galaxy, Seventh Dimension

6049 Y.Y. (Yessat Years)

"It's okay," Kari Gy'at Li murmured. Her warm, silver-blue gaze studied the young princess's tight features. Kari felt sure Dari had come so close to confiding in her, but when the princess had opened her mouth to speak…

Nothing. Only silence and a haunted stare.

The girl wasn't just scared — she was terrified. Whatever it was that Princess Dari Q'ana Tal knew, whatever secret she had been harboring since she'd fled to the matriarchal planet of Galis, it was more burden than any one person should bear alone.

Kari sighed. She understood the toll of living with secrets all too well. Dari's stoic features served as a mirror, reflecting back to Kari her own need for self-preservation at all costs. For years she had pretended to be someone she wasn't, a fact none but her adopted sisters knew. The cost of staying alive in this once-foreign world had come at the price of forsaking who she really was.

Forgetting, however, was another animal altogether. It simply wasn't possible. She could pretend, she could keep the memories locked away in the farthest recesses of her mind as best she could, but they never really left her. Nor did she want them to.

"My real name isn't Kari," she softly admitted. "And I wasn't born to the Gy'at Lis." The princess slowly craned her neck, her glowing blue eyes wide, as she stared at her with rapt interest. Kari told herself she was about to spill her heart out to her traveling companion merely to break the ice and hopefully win her confidence. Maybe if she shared one of her secrets with Dari, the princess would realize she could trust her with one of her own. Tit for tat, a secret for a secret. It was a fair exchange. "Surely you can tell just by looking at me that I'm not even from Galis."

As the admission left her lips, she gave up the self-imposed charade. This was more than an attempt at manipulation and she knew it. She was going to tell Dari who she was and where she was from because she actually wanted to. They could very well be butchered after their gastrolight cruiser landed on Khan-Gor. She didn't want to go to her death still pretending.

"You are jesting," Dari weakly returned. "For a certainty you speak in riddles and you—"

"Do I sound like a Galian? Do I even look like one?"

The princess was quiet for a protracted moment. "Nay." Dari visibly swallowed as she trained her gaze on her lap. "You have the look of—" Her voice, a smoky feminine sound that slightly reverberated when she spoke, lowered to a mumble. "'Tis not important."

Kari's wine-red eyebrows drew together. "What do you mean? Who do I have the look of?"

"'Tis naught but the musings of a weary mind."

"But—"

"Leastways," Dari interrupted, abruptly surging to her feet. "I should check on Bazi."

Kari sighed as she watched the princess hurry away. The sleeping male child Dari had fled Arak with and brought to Galis had been looked in on less than five *Nuba*-minutes past. Indeed, ever since the three of them had made a hasty departure from Kari's adopted home, narrowly escaping capture from the warriors who would stop at nothing to reclaim their runaway princess, Dari had conveniently needed to check on Bazi every time the two women got close to confiding in each other.

She absently looked through the gastrolight cruiser's transparent front window, her gaze raking over the ice-coated planet of Khan-Gor. She wasn't altogether certain why the urge to tell the princess everything was so strong. At first she had believed it to be out of a sense of camaraderie, a desire to grow closer to the young royal now that they were all the other had. Yet there was more to it, something she couldn't quite put her finger on.

Maybe it was simply the fact that the princess reminded her of Geris, her real sister's lifelong best friend. The resemblance between them was uncanny. Were it not for the fact it was next to impossible…

She shook her head slightly, as if attempting to erase that ludicrous thought from her mind Etch-a-Sketch style. The strikingly beautiful Dari possessed Geris' dark mahogany coloring and her regal, statuesque bearing — hell, the princess even wore her hair like Geris had in a veil of long, black microbraids that hung to her waist — but the similarities ended once you gazed into her eyes. Dari's glowing blue orbs were a reminder of the alien civilization Kari'd been whisked away to so many years ago, whereas Geris' earthy brown eyes had bespoken of home.

"What is your true name?" Dari whispered, startling Kari. She'd been so lost in thought she hadn't realized her companion had returned. "From whence do you come?"

Kari took a deep breath and slowly expelled it. A soft smile tugged at her lips as her gaze found Dari's. Finally—*finally*—the princess was dropping her shield, or at least lowering it enough to let her in a bit. They had another three days of travel before the spaceship would breach Khan-Gor, the legendary Planet of the Predators. The only certainty they had now was each other.

She needed to know Dari's secret before that third day arrived or she couldn't protect them from whatever evil the princess feared dwelled there. The only way to gain her confidence was to give her hers first. Trust didn't come easy for either one of them—a shared trait that was undoubtedly responsible for keeping them both alive this long.

The irony was not lost on her. The same steel-willed resolve that had permitted survival would ultimately destroy them if they didn't let it go. Kari had understood this for several days; she realized Dari now did as well. Revealing her past to anyone but the Gy'at Lis had been unthinkable up to this point, yet now here she sat, yearning to tell the princess who she was and where she was from.

"My name is Kara," she breathed out for the first time in more years than she could remember. It felt so good to taste her real name on her tongue as it escaped from between her parted lips. "Kara Summers."

Chapter One

Orlando, Florida - First Dimension

July 4, 1999 A.D. (Anno Domini)

"What the hell am I doing here?"

Kara Summers muttered the question to herself as she glanced around the amusement park she had unenthusiastically agreed to attend today. Seated at a picnic table next to a hotdog stand, she plopped her chin on her palm and contemplated why she'd allowed Jonathon to drag her here in the first place. Or more to the point, she thought glumly, why was she dating a grown man with no kids who considered *this* a good time?

Disney World. Her lips pinched together in a frown. If this was the happiest place on earth, humanity was fucked.

Kara decided the fault could be placed at the feet of her older sister, Kyra, for this debacle. She had, after all, talked her into going out with Jonathon in the first place. , Kyra had described Jonathon, a fellow accountant at her sister's firm, as settled, ready for a commitment, and financially solid.

In other words, boring.

"That Spaceship Earth ride was totally rad!" Jonathon enthused. Kara blinked. She hadn't heard him approach over the sound of her self-pity. He plopped a paper bowl down in front of her that contained a hotdog, French fries, and several ketchup packets. The lemonade came next. "Let's try the Pirates of the Caribbean ride after we eat."

Let's try a suicide pact and hang ourselves.

"Well..." Her irritation slowly gave way to guilt. Feeling like the bitch her last boyfriend had called her, she forced a semi-smile to her lips. Jonathon was a good guy. He simply wasn't turning out to be the guy for her. Fortunately, she could tell he wasn't getting "the vibe" either so it wasn't as if ending things would break his heart. Jonathon was no doubt simply trying to make the best of things until they returned to New York City tomorrow. It wouldn't kill her to do the same. "Sure. Sounds like fun."

She supposed the suicide pact could wait. Besides, being a natural redhead with skin the color of porcelain, she'd probably sizzle like a vampire before hanging herself became an issue. Disney World in July. What had she been thinking? Colonizing the planet Mercury would have been less painful.

Kara opened a ketchup packet and squirted out the contents onto her fries. "Spaceship Earth was pretty interesting, if a little farfetched."

"Agreed." Jonathon pushed his glasses further up the bridge of his nose with one finger. "As if we'll ever be able to talk to people in real-time while seeing them simultaneously. Utterly absurd."

"Maybe a few generations from now, but we won't be alive to see it."

"Exactly." He bit off a large piece of hotdog and talked while chewing it. Kara winced. "It would be cool if we did though."

She glanced down to her plate and eyed her hotdog. She had a phobia about seeing food bits in people's mouths. Better to stare at her hotdog than to dry-heave. "Totally."

They ate in silence for the next several minutes. The quiet gave Kara time to contemplate what her next course of action should be. Should she state the obvious and tell him that she'd like to be his friend, but wasn't interested in more? Or just forgo the conversation altogether and let their lack of mutual attraction speak for itself?

"I need to admit something to you, Kara, and it isn't easy."

Her head shot up. One wine-red eyebrow arched quizzically. Was he about to do the hard part for her and tell her she wasn't the woman for him? Good lord she hoped so. "Okay."

"It's just..." He cleared his throat and fumbled with a napkin. "I don't want to hurt you."

Hurt me. Please. "Go on."

Jonathon's mouth worked up and down, but no words were coming out of it. Just say it already! Then we can officially be "just friends" and maybe halfway enjoy this dumbass place. "I...uhhh...I..."

She feigned patience she wasn't feeling. "Whatever it is, just say —"

"I'm gay."

Silence. Her mouth dropped open. *She* wasn't the woman for him? Damn. Apparently there was no woman for him.

Kara blinked. She prided herself on her remarkable gaydar, but she hadn't seen that one coming. He didn't work out at the gym and had zero fashion sense. He ate with his mouth open for shit's sake. "Are you sure?" she said dumbly.

"I'm sorry, but yes."

She couldn't have been happier if she actively tried to be. Her smile was radiant. Relieved and radiant. "There's no need to be sorry!"

"There isn't?"

"No way." Her expression grew serious as concern took over. "But why are you in the closet?"

"My family," he sighed.

"Ah." Her silver-blue gaze filled with compassion. "I understand, Jonathon, but they'll come around eventually."

"I don't know about that."

"Then they don't deserve to have you in their lives," she said firmly. Kara splayed her hands. "You only go around once. You deserve to be happy while you're doing it."

Jonathon showed his first hint of a smile. "Thank you."

Kara nodded. "If you need the support of a friend, I'll be happy to stand by your side while you tell them."

"I appreciate that, but I think this is something I need to do alone."

"I understand, but the offer still stands if you change your mind."

His smile was genuine. "Thank you."

From that point on their conversation no longer felt stilted. It actually became fun. They talked about everything from politics, to who they thought would win today's Wimbledon (Kara was rooting for Steffi Graf), to the new Harry Potter book releasing in a few days.

"Come on," Kara said, standing. "Let's grab two Mickey Mouse ice-cream bars and eat them on the way to that Pirates of the Caribbean ride."

"I'm hungry for one of those chocolate-covered frozen bananas."

Kara grinned. She couldn't resist teasing him. "I bet you are."

Jonathon laughed.

* * * * *

Climbing into the wooden boat with another twenty or so tourists, Kara found herself feeling grateful for the respite a water ride would provide from such a hot day. As the boat lurched forward, one of several children on board stood up and shouted, "Whoop whoop!"

"Sit down!" his mother chastised, tugging at his shirt. She held a toddler in her lap. "You'll get us kicked off the ride."

Kara doubted such was possible since their boat had already taken off, but the threat worked. The wide-eyed boy looked around for any signs of a Disney worker prepared to yank him off the ride. He settled into his seat.

The next several minutes were, well, boring, but the cool air-conditioning more than made up for the very unconvincing animatronic pirates. The boat lurched upward, beginning its ascent up a track.

"There's a small fall at the end of this ride," Jonathon whispered. "It's fun."

"You've been on this before?"

"What can I say? I'm a kid at heart."

She half snorted and half laughed. "Nothing wrong with that."

The boat reached the apex, signaling the approach of a rapid descent. It was no log ride, but she conceded a little bit of fast movement down the hill would serve to pep things up a bit.

"All right!" the little kid who couldn't seem to sit still yelled out. "Here we go, Mommy!"

Kara's eyes widened as the little boy surged to his feet at the worst possible moment. Her stomach leapt into her throat when she realized his mother was too busy caring for the toddler to notice her older son. Time seemed to pass in slow motion as the boat raced down the hill, the boy still standing.

Kara leapt out of her seat, grabbed the child by the back of the shirt and pulled him down. He fell to the floor of the boat, stunned but okay. Kara cried out as she tried to regain her footing, her heart pounding in her chest. Jonathon's eyes widened in horror as he reached out a helping hand a moment too late. She screamed as her body lost its battle with gravity and plummeted into the cold, deep water.

A sharp pain splintered through Kara's head as she hit the bottom of the tank. Desperate, frightened, and knowing she'd be crushed if she didn't breach the surface and get out of the water before the next boat came barreling down the track, her arms and legs instinctively flailed.

A bright light blindsided Kara, rendering her disoriented. Unable to distinguish up from down, she could do nothing but hold her breath while she awaited the next boat's impact.

I'm a dead woman. No one can survive this.

Her body felt as if it were moving faster than a tsunami, which she knew wasn't possible. Dizzy and terrified, she hysterically decided this must be how people get to Heaven…or to Hell. She continued to hold her breath as her body whizzed through space and time. She hoped she awoke to the sight of angels rather than demons.

The happiest place on earth, my ass.

Chapter Two

The Matriarchal Planet of Galis

Trek Mi Q'an Galaxy, Seventh Dimension

6022 Y.Y. (Yessat Years)

Kara coughed and sputtered as her head pierced the water's surface. Her lungs ached from holding her breath, but the need for air was tantamount. She sucked in as much oxygen as was possible, her throat and lungs burning from the successive, harsh gasps.

Get it under control. You've got to get out of this tank before the next boat smashes you into oblivion!

Panting, gasping, and coughing, Kara fought to steady herself. It took her lungs another full minute of dragging in air before they were replete. Her head was aching and her eyes burning, but she needed to know where she was in proximity to the oncoming boat in order to get out of its way before doing so became a moot point. She wasn't dead and she wanted to keep it that way.

Kara forced her gaze open despite the searing pain. She blinked several times in rapid succession, her eyes taking what felt like forever to adjust.

An odd feeling stole over her, a sixth sense that told Kara something wasn't right. It dawned on her that she wasn't hearing any of the sounds that should be assaulting her senses right about now—no boisterous children, no shouts of mad panic as workers attempted to pull her from the tank...

No nothing.

She fought with her vision, mentally demanding it to bring her surroundings into focus. When her eyes at last obeyed, she felt more disoriented than she had when her world had been a blur. "What the—"

Kara's eyes widened in disbelief. Her gaze frantically darted around. "I must be dead," she muttered, too shocked to become hysterical. "This isn't happening."

Treading in water that resembled a liquefied mirror, she gaped at the maroon shore just ahead. Beyond the shore lay a dense jungle, its trees and plant-life a slightly darker shade of reddish-purple. Rising above the thick foliage was a series of austere black mountains. Innumerable white structures that looked crystal in appearance encircled the foothills of the obsidian massifs, while a single, palatial edifice of purple crystal sat at the apex of each peak.

Kara closed her eyes tightly. "I'm hallucinating or I'm dreaming. I must be in a coma or something."

Maybe she'd swum into a back lot and was viewing what would eventually be a new Disney ride. With all the purple and crystal it was possibly some ostentatious tribute to The Artist Formerly Known as Prince. Or to Liberace.

She wanted to believe either of those scenarios, but a nagging feeling in the pit of her belly told her it just wasn't so. Her eyes flew back open and her gaze wandered up further still, beyond the purple mansions and into the bluest skies she'd ever before seen. They looked as if they'd been colored in with crayons.

She stilled, the hair at the nape of her neck standing on end. Kara stared unblinking at a sight so alien, so unbelievable, that she couldn't be certain it was even real. Five moons of varying color dipped down from the heavens, piercing the blue skyline beneath them. "Where am I?" she whispered, goose bumps forming on her skin. "What the hell is happening?"

If she wasn't dead and she wasn't dreaming then only one possibility remained, but that prospect was so farfetched as to be unthinkable. Kara swallowed past the lump in her throat, her silver-blue gaze paradoxically vacant and haunted. Her heart slammed in her chest as she wondered aloud, "Am I still on Earth?"

A gigantic flying monkey swooped down from the mountains, carrying two women on its back. Kara sucked in her breath while the females eyed her quizzically, as if she was as foreign to them as all this was to her.

Her mind was too stunned to perform even the most basic of motor skills—like moving her arms and legs. No longer treading water, it briefly occurred to Kara that the middle of a mirror-like body of water wasn't exactly the most ideal of places to experience the first fainting spell of her life. As quickly as that thought struck her, blackness engulfed her.

* * * * *

"A fe'ka myna?"

"Zoot f'ya!"

"Ba ti fe'ka."

Kara slowly opened her eyes, her eyelashes batting away any remaining vestiges of sleep fainting had provided. Two female faces hovered over her. Two foreign faces with caramel-mocha coloring, long dark hair and... *violet eyes*?

She sighed. If these women were Prince groupies they were taking his love of purple to a new extreme.

"*A fe'ka myna?*" one of the women half asked and half demanded.

Kara's nose wrinkled as she met the woman's — violet! — gaze. Whoever the stranger was, she was definitely the most authoritative of the duo. "I don't understand what you're asking me..." Her voice trailed off as she noticed what the foreigners were wearing. Kara's breath hitched and her eyes rounded. "You're naked!" she sputtered, sitting up. "Or close enough to naked to freak me out!"

Both of the strange-speaking, strange-looking women wore G-strings, sandals with straps that wound up and crisscrossed around each leg to just below the knee, and nothing else. They looked like slutty prostitutes from Roman days gone by. Or like members of some psychedelic harem Prince had put together. Kara's eyes narrowed into silver-blue slits. He had another think coming if the Purple Pain thought she would dress like that, wear violet contact lenses, and learn some trippy language he'd invented. He was as weird as legend allowed, she thought grimly.

The dominant of the duo reached down and touched Kara's erect nipple. She gasped, unaware until that moment she was more naked than either of them. "What are you doing?" she breathed out. "Where am I? Please don't —"

But they weren't paying her any attention. Speaking in that bizarre language, they talked to each other without paying her any mind. They behaved as though they'd never seen the pink nipples of a redhead before. The leader rolled her nipple around, watching with rapt interest when it lengthened and darkened. Kara swallowed, wishing the duo wasn't so convincing in their surprise.

The other stranger's hand found her other nipple and played with it too. The arousal Kara felt was sudden and horrifying. She lifted her hands to push theirs away when an inexplicable fatigue consumed her. She fell back down, her head hitting the softest pillow she'd ever felt. Her arms collapsed to either side of her nude body. She dug her nails into the silky, palatial bed she'd awoken on.

What was happening? These women, whoever they were, weren't Prince groupies. She couldn't say how she knew, yet she did. Kara's thoughts returned to the five moons that dipped below the sky and hovered above the mirror-silver waters. The maroon landscape and jungle. The black mountains and crystalline purple palaces perched at the apexes...

Kara wasn't on Earth. Acceptance of that fact should have made her hysterical, but haziness stole over her instead. Had the women drugged her? She'd never tried LSD, but this was as close to understanding Pink Floyd's *The Wall* as she'd likely ever get.

Her fingers, once gripping the whisper-soft bed covers for dear life, fell limp. She had to have been drugged. There was no other explanation.

All this for a little kid on a Disney ride who wouldn't listen to his mother. Shit.

* * * * *

Klykka Gy'at Li, High Mystik of the sector that bore her surname, stared down at the alien creature she and her sisters had saved from drowning in the waters of Loch Valor. The female was unlike any other The Gy'at Li had ever afore seen. Leastways, her hair was the color of fire-berries and her eyes the shade of the leaves of a *jumyun* tree. 'Twas strange, that. Beautiful, but unusual. Odder still, the female sported a small triangular patch of hair on her pussy that was identical in shade to the hair upon her head. Galian women didn't grow hair on their pussies and in all her *Yessat* years Klykka had never heard tell of a species of females that did. And the creature's skin…'twas reminiscent of the creamy colored milk Galians drank from the purple fruits of the *Trefa* jungle.

Klykka's nose wrinkled. 'Twas an enigma, this one. In all the galaxies of the four dimensions she'd traded in, made war against, and visited for a time, never had she seen a female who carried the look of this one. By the time a female earned the rank of High Mystik she'd seen and done it all. Or so she'd thought.

"She doesn't speak Galian or any other language known to me," Dorra said.

Klykka didn't look away from the alien female as she replied to her sister. "Nor any known to myself."

"You think her a *Kefa* slave of Tryston or a bound servant mayhap?"

"Nay. She hasn't the look of the slaves and she was wearing odd clothing when we removed her from the loch."

Dorra grunted her agreement. "Aye. Bound servants are kept mostly naked."

Klykka had been inspecting the female creature ever since she'd placed her upon the *vesha*-hide bed. The alien was beautiful, her visage exotic, yet she was useless to their sector should she be unable to reach thought-lock with her and the female warriors she ruled o'er. Thought-lock was a rarely used weapon, but 'twas a crucial one.

"What should we do with her? Mayhap she is dumb of the mind, Klykka."

"Mayhap."

"Should I take her to the gulch pits and offer her as a sacrifice to the goddess?"

"I cannot say." The Gy'at Li sighed. "And there's only one way to find out."

* * * * *

Kara fought the intense, gnawing arousal with every bit of strength she had left. Her treasonous nipples stabbed out, her body betraying her. She wanted to scream—from fear or pleasure she could no longer say. Her eyelids shuttered, opening slightly, letting her take in the scene unfolding for a brief moment.

Her surroundings still hazy, her body adrift in a sea of arousal, the two alien females kissed and licked all over her. Kara gasped, the first sound to escape her lips since this foreign fog had enveloped her. If the women hadn't been totally naked before, they were now.

The dominant female's caramel-colored hands reached for Kara's porcelain-pale knees. Their gazes clashed and locked. The leader thrust Kara's legs apart, a half-smile curving her red lips. The alien's face, so perfect in every way, disappeared between her thighs.

Kara gasped again, her eyes closing and her head lolling back, the feel of a soft tongue swiping across her clit. She moaned, her hips instinctively rearing up to give the stranger full access to her pussy. The second woman positioned herself next to Kara and played with her stiff nipples, tweaking and sucking on them as the first female continued to swig at her clit. Kara groaned loudly, a knot of titillation coiling in her belly.

There were hands and tongues all over her, hundreds of them, rubbing and licking and sucking, coaxing her flesh into an intense state of arousal. Her eyes flew open. There were only two women touching her, yet she felt hands and tongues everywhere. Both of her nipples were being sucked, her clit nuzzled, her anus tickled, her ears kissed...

Kara came on a loud moan, her eyes closing, as the hardest orgasm she'd ever known slammed through her body. Her orgasm created a ripple effect, causing the other two females to come as well. The power of their mirroring orgasms turned the ripple into a tidal wave. Kara screamed as another wave of primal hedonism ripped through her, her breathing turning into pants.

And then another wave came, and another, each orgasm stronger than the last. Her skin was slick with perspiration, her clit pulsing, her nipples so stiff they ached. "No more!" she begged, exhausted. She was so drained of energy and fluid that she feared dehydration. "Please—no more!"

A final orgasm hit her, its impact a tsunami. Kara moaned like an animal as she rode out the wave. A blinding flash of light slammed through her head, the pain worse than any she'd ever felt. She could hear the two females chanting, the dominant one demanding entrance into her mind. She instinctively recoiled against it, but the leader's will was stronger. Exhausted and whimpering, Kara gave up whatever fight she had left in her. She closed her eyes and succumbed.

A fe'ka myna?

A fe'ka myna?

Kara's mind entered an inexplicable void that she shared with this strange woman. The void quickly cracked, scaring her, as the mirror-like waters rushed in. Her heart rate accelerated. The stranger held out her hands.

A fe'ka myna?

Trembling, Kara grasped her offered hands. Beneath an endless sea of liquefied mirror, they should have been drowning.

What fe'ka myna?

But they weren't drowning. And she instinctively understood that she would never drown so long as she trusted in this alien woman. Kara's heart rate calmed.

What is your myna?

Her silver-blue gaze locked with the stranger's violet one. Kara squeezed her hands tighter.

What is your name?

Her eyes widened and her lips trembled, but she opened her mouth and spoke. She had no idea where she was or how she'd gotten here, but she knew all the answers would be soon in coming.

My name is Kara Summers.

Chapter Three

Kara awoke on a yawn, her tummy growling as she stretched her muscles. Today marked a full Yessat year since she'd arrived on the planet Galis. She smiled, knowing her adoptive family had planned a day of festivities to mark the anniversary. But first she needed breakfast.

Naked, Kara climbed out of her cozy bed and donned a blue *zoka*—a garment that amounted to nothing more than a shiny G-string. She chose matching blue sandals with ribbons that crisscrossed up her calves and tied just below the knee to complete her wardrobe. Her breasts were bare, as was expected. No Galian female ever shielded them from the eyes of others.

It had taken Kara several months to accustom herself to the norms of this world, but she was proud of herself for having done so. Nakedness was no longer equated with embarrassment and vulnerability in her thinking, but with pride and empowerment.

As she walked down the crystal corridor and headed toward the spiral staircase that would take her to the great room and dining hall below, she reflected on how different her life had become since arriving on Galis. Like Alice tumbling through the rabbit hole and into Wonderland, Kara had been whisked through space and time by forces unknown into a world that made little sense to her earthly mind. The pieces of the puzzle were slowly coming together, but learning was an ongoing process that would take years — if not the rest of her life — to completely comprehend.

Some of the knowledge had been quick in coming, especially as it applied to gender roles. On Galis, social interactions and political processes were dictated by female mystiks rather than by the whims of wealthy men. Here it was women who ruled and males who deferred to the "goddess-given superiority of females" in all matters. Galian women were bred to lead; Galian men were reared to follow. The unfortunate result for a transplanted female Earthling was a lack of attraction to the weepy, sensitive, sexually manipulative ways of the effeminate Galian males. What Klykka and Dorra found arousing about Galian men were the very things that turned Kara off. Despite their muscular physicality and six-foot statures they were, quite frankly, wimps.

"There you are," Klykka said, smiling from her seat at the head of the dining hall's table. Kara's naked breasts jiggled as she made her way down the staircase. "I was about to send a servant to locate you."

"I must have been exhausted from last night's lessons because I slept like a baby."

"'Tis tiring, your training." Klykka nodded her understanding. "Mayhap we should continue at a slower pace."

"No way!" Kara took her seat next to Klykka, directly across the table from Dorra. She threw an absent look at the naked male standing stoically behind her chair, prepared to serve Kara in whatever capacity arose. His cock, perpetually stiffened by a spell Klykka had placed on all male servants under The Gy'at Li's dominion, was as erect as ever. The Galian version of a moist towelette dangled from his penis. At meal's end it was considered proper to use the towelette to clean one's hands.

Kara sighed. It had been a year and she still wasn't accustomed to that particular facet of Galian life. Stiff erections aside, the concepts of magic and casting spells were the stuff of sideshow carnivals back on earth. But here? They weren't merely concepts or tricks used to fool a rapt audience — they were real and they worked.

"Happy day of birth, sister," Dorra told her. She raised a chalice of fermented *pici* juice. "'Tis proud I am to call you a Gy'at Li."

Kara's smile was soft and genuine. Dorra hadn't exactly been her biggest fan when Klykka made the choice to adopt her as a blood-sister, but Kara had worked her butt off to gain Dorra's trust and approval since day one. It had paid off. She knew Dorra had come to love her as Klykka did. "Thank you. I'm very proud to bear your name."

"Speaking of names," Klykka announced, drawing Kara's attention, "'tis a pity this must be done today on your Galian day of birth, but it must."

Kara's wine-red eyebrows drew together.

"I must choose for you a new name," Klykka informed her. "Leastways, you cannot be called 'Kara' ever again."

Kara's gaze widened. She immediately felt sick to her stomach. The last remaining vestige of her home, of her family, was being stripped from her? "Why?" she asked, breathless. "It's all I have left from—"

"We know, sister," Dorra interjected. Her violet eyes were uncharacteristically empathetic. Dorra wasn't prone toward showing emotion—any emotion. "But 'tis the holy law."

"I don't understand..."

Klykka's bare breasts heaved on an expulsion of air. "Our planet is a part of the Trek Mi Q'an galaxy," she explained, "and as such we must abide by its laws. Whilst the emperor is content to not interfere in Galian politics or our way of life, 'tis with the understanding that we adhere to his galactic decrees."

"He doesn't make many," Dorra muttered, "but when he does they must be obeyed."

Kara shook her head. "I still don't understand what my name has to do with this emperor or a holy law."

"No humanoid within Trek Mi Q'an can share the same name as the emperor, empress, or any in their direct bloodline of succession." Klykka handed her a parchment. Judging by the laser stamp on the broken seal, the communiqué had likely just been delivered. "Each time a new hatchling is born to the emperor a missive is sent out to all rulers of the planets under his power declaring the royal child's name."

"Once that happens," Dorra interjected, "the decree is then circulated to the lesser rulers who in turn disperse it to the free men and women of their protection."

"All who carry the name of the new royal hatchling are given no choice but to change their names." Klykka frowned. She picked up her chalice of *pici* juice. "'Tis that or the gulch pits of Kogar."

Kara scanned the royal missive. She had learned to read, write and speak several languages by joining Klykka in a lesser version of thought-lock known as linking. Trystonni, the native tongue of the emperor, was one of them. Her heart sank as her eyes zeroed in on the pertinent part of the decree:

In the Yessat Year of the Goddess 6023, on the seventh day of light in the moon-month of Rama, the Empress of Trek Mi Q'an and High Queen of Tryston did so hatch the High Princess Kara Q'ana Tal...

Kara's nostrils flared. She crumpled up the parchment as she fought back the tears that threatened to spill. The only thing a person ever truly owned was their name. Now she didn't even have that. And all because some bitch on another planet hatched a baby?

Hatched a baby? What the— She stilled. That question would have to wait.

"'Tis sorry we are, sister," Klykka said softly. She covered Kara's hand with her own. "I would that I could defy this directive, yet I cannot. 'Twould put the whole of my sector in harm's way."

"I understand," Kara whispered. "I don't like it, but I understand."

"In truth," Dorra frowned, covering Kara's free hand with hers, "'twould be wondrous to me did we declare war on the warriors of Tryston. Their way of life is perverse."

"Aye." Klykka nodded her agreement. "Women serving men, wives living in total subjugation to their Sacred Mates…" She harrumphed. "'Tis as natural as hatching a babe from your arse."

Kara's amusement came out as a snort. "Thanks for the mental image." She grinned, her dimples popping out. "I guess I'll never be vacationing on Tryston."

The sisters released Kara's hands and told her frightening tales about the Trystonni warriors. They stood seven to eight feet in height, had heavily muscled bodies, were the fiercest of fighters, and had a reputation for stealing women they coveted as brides. It was the stuff nightmares were made of. The males of Galis might be too emotional for Kara's taste, but at least they weren't misogynist assholes with an affinity for kidnapping.

"Many warriors travel to Galis. They are bedazzled from childhood onward by stories of our mastery in the sexual arts." Klykka's face was stern. "'Tis mayhap impossible to avoid the Trystonni warriors altogether, but 'tis for a certainty you should never share the *vesha* hides with one."

"Several Galian females have gone missing throughout the Yessat Years," Dorra murmured, "and always after sharing the *vesha* hides with a warrior. Do not join their numbers, sister."

Kara's eyes widened. The women sat in silence for a prolonged moment as Kara's brain soaked up all she'd just learned. She took a sip of *pici* juice, the lump in her throat making swallowing a bit difficult.

"Well then," Kara finally said, setting down her chalice. She didn't want to give up her name for it reminded her of the home she could never return to—and the sister she'd never again see. Not a day went by that she didn't grieve the loss of Kyra. But neither did she wish to draw the attention of the warriors from planet Tryston, much less incur their wrath. "I guess you better tell me what my new name is then."

Klykka nodded. She could tell by her expression that The Gy'at Li was proud Kara hadn't given into the desire to weep. Emotionalism was expected in males, but frowned upon in females, especially women training under a High Mystik.

Kara'd been caught crying a few times since arriving on Galis, mostly at night when she thought she was alone and had permitted herself to think about her sister. She could only pray Kyra had moved on in life rather than mourn her. With their parents dead, all they'd had left was each other and Geris—her sister's best friend since childhood. If there was any consolation to be had, it was in knowing that Kyra would always have Geris by her side.

The High Mystik's chin notched up. Her violet gaze was simultaneously soft and firm. "I bestow upon you the name Kari," Klykka announced. "Kari Gy'at Li."

Chapter Four

Three Moon-risings Outside Khan-Gori Airspace
Zyrus Galaxy, Seventh Dimension
6049 Y.Y. (Yessat Years)

"You're looking at me as if I just sprouted three heads," Kari mused, her silver-blue gaze trained on Dari. "Surely out of all the crazy things that go on in Trek Mi Q'an my life story isn't the craziest."

"N-not at all," Dari sputtered. Her glowing blue eyes were wide, her hands fidgeting in her lap. Kari didn't know what to make of that. "I just…"

"Yeah? You just what?"

"I just need to check on Bazi." She soared to her feet. "Leastways, 'tis a lot to take in, your story."

Kari frowned as she watched the princess walk toward the Arakian boy's sleeping quarters. Every time Dari got nervous or close to confiding in her, she immediately used Bazi as an excuse to remove herself from the situation. *That* Kari was used to, but Dari staring at her as if she'd seen a ghost was a new phenomenon altogether.

Three days and three nights—that was all they had left before their gastrolight cruiser breached Khan-Gor's airspace.

And the clock, Kari conceded as she checked the spaceship's readings, was ticking. In four mere *Nuba*-hours, three days and three nights would become three days and two nights. Time was of the essence for it was no longer on their side.

"Please finish your story," the princess said as she came back to the front of the ship. She was carrying a tray of food and *matpow*—a delicious fermented drink that reminded her of the mead she'd once tried back home at a medieval fair. "I need to hear the whole of it before I speak on this."

One of Kari's eyebrows inched up. Dari was hiding something—and that something had nothing to do with the evil that awaited them on Khan-Gor. Kari's reminiscing had caused the young royal's face to blanch, which made no sense. She accepted a chalice of *matpow* from Dari as she studied the princess' schooled features.

"All right," Kari slowly agreed. She recognized that no answers would be forthcoming from Dari until she finished her story. "I'll tell you the rest."

Hopefully then, at long last, the princess would trust her.

Chapter Five

The Matriarchal Planet of Galis
Trek Mi Q'an Galaxy, Seventh Dimension
6039 Y.Y. (Yessat Years)

Seventeen Yessat Years had gone by since the day Kari emerged from the silver-mirror waters of Loch Valor. She tried not to think about the fact her sister had been dead for hundreds, possibly thousands of years, but every anniversary of her arrival on Galis brought the knowledge and resulting grief to the forefront of her consciousness.

In the seventh dimension of Trek Mi Q'an galaxy, time didn't function as it did back on Earth. The days were much longer and the months more plentiful. Klykka had tried to do the math once, but because she'd never trekked to the first dimension of time and space where Earth dwelled it was difficult to estimate how many Earth years went by with the passing of a single Yessat Year. *"Between ten to one hundred, sister, depending upon the year. 'Tis the best calculation I can give you for time works differently in each dimension."*

Ten, fifty, one hundred...it really didn't matter. Any way Kari looked at it, her sister and Geris had been long dead. That fact was not only difficult to grasp, it was also downright depressing.

Had her sister ever married? Did she have children? Had her life been a happy one? These were the questions that plagued Kari whenever she allowed herself to remember, to feel, so she rarely indulged them.

Standing on the maroon shores of Loch Valor, Kari Gy'at Li stared into the waters that had brought her here so many Yessat Years ago. She usually avoided this place like the plague, but today was the anniversary of her departure from Earth. Once a year she made this pilgrimage; once a year she allowed herself to mourn the loss of her former self and the accompanying memories that made up who she had once been.

"I will never forget you, Kyra," she murmured. "Wherever you are, whatever form your spirit has taken on, I will always love you." She swiped away a rogue tear. "I miss you so fucking much." Taking a deep breath and slowly exhaling, Kari forced a smile to her lips. "Tell Geris I'm sorry I wrecked her Mercedes that time I borrowed it. It still bothers me that I blamed it on that poor valet guy." She shook her head slightly. "I realize the futility of regret, but there it is nonetheless."

Kari sighed as she took note of her image in the silvery waters. The liquid cast back such an accurate reflection that all Galian mirrors were made from it. Indeed, it was one of the planet's biggest exports. Today her likeness echoed back a spectacle that even the Gy'at Li couldn't explain—nobody, or at least nobody in Trek Mi Q'an galaxy, ever aged.

Seventeen Yessat Years had passed and Kari looked no different now than she had upon her arrival. Had she never been brought here and seventeen Earth years had ticked by, her appearance would reflect that of a middle-aged woman rather than a girl in her twenties. Nothing was the same on Galis. Here she was barely considered a woman. Truly, her adoptive sisters treated her much like a child. Given that Klykka and Dorra had both been alive for hundreds of Yessat Years, she supposed she still was by their way of thinking.

"I love you, Kyra," Kari whispered. She indulged in a final teary moment before batting away the moisture from her eyelashes. "I'll see you next year, Sis."

* * * * *

"'Tis a proficient pack-hunter you've become," Klykka told Kari before picking up her chalice and sipping from it. "Leastways, every Yessat Year that passes by makes me prouder of your accomplishments."

Kari beamed at the rare praise. Finished eating, she grabbed the towelette from the erection closest to her without breaking eye contact with her sister. "Thank you." She dabbed at her lips, clearing away the remaining juices of the succulent, roasted *vesha* beast they'd just dined on. "That means a lot coming from you."

"'Tis true, her words," Dorra confirmed. "Never did I think you would surpass even myself at bagging and tagging. Leastways, you have."

Bagging and tagging. Sweet lord above if Kyra could have watched *that* ritual unfold! Her birth sister's reaction would have been priceless. The mental image of Kyra's shocked expression amused her. She picked up her chalice and sipped from it to keep from smiling, not wanting Dorra to think she was making fun of her.

"What amuses you, sister?" Klykka asked.

Kari's eyes widened. So much for her attempt at camouflage. Deciding to be honest, she told her adoptive sisters what she'd been thinking. It didn't take long before all three of them were grinning.

"What was courtship and mating like on Earth?" Dorra asked. Her violet gaze perfectly matched the *zoka* she'd chosen to wear today. "You do not hunt men and men do not hunt women?" Her expression was confused. "How in the sands does anyone ever take a mate to the marriage bed?"

Kari couldn't help but laugh. She supposed the earthly way of matrimony would seem odd to a people who took whom they wanted by force.

None of the Gy'at Lis had married yet. Klykka and Dorra regularly engaged in sex with all the male servants, but neither had an interest in marrying any time soon. When they were ready, they would pick virgin males from the marriage auction block or pack-hunt their grooms by themselves.

Bagging and tagging was how the female warriors of the Gy'at Li sector earned credits. Working in teams, they pack-hunted virgin Galian males to sell to prospective mistresses — brides — at the auction block. The bigger and more cunning the male, the more exorbitant his asking price was. Yesterday on the auction block in Valor City, they had sold every single male they'd bagged on their last pack-hunt. The planet's capital seat, Valor City attracted wealthy female buyers from sectors all across Galis.

Even though the entire ritual was collectively referred to as bagging and tagging, the pack-hunters only did the bagging part, the capturing. The tagging, or branding of one's mate, was done by the bride herself after she purchased him.

Yes, Kari mused, grinning, Kyra would have pissed her pants from shock watching that shit go down.

"On Earth, some couples are bound to each other without their consent by the bride's and groom's parents. We call that an 'arranged marriage'."

"Without the bride's consent?" Dorra asked incredulously.

"*Especially* without the bride's consent. The groom may or may not have some say-so in the decision."

Dorra's expression was grim. "'Tis a perversion of nature, that."

"Aye," Klykka concurred. "They must share the *vesha* hides with a male not of their choosing?"

Kari nodded. "When I left Earth arranged marriages were only common in certain parts of the planet. There was a time when almost all marriages were arranged, but that was long before I was born."

"For a certainty would I flee," Dorra muttered on a grunt. "And slay any who would try to stop me."

Kari decided now wasn't the time to explain how lowly women were regarded in certain parts of Earth—or how fleeing nearly always resulted in the female's death. She'd save that sad tale for another day. Besides, Dorra already looked primed to start a war. "Luckily, most marriages where I'm from are a result of two people falling in love and deciding they want to spend the rest of their lives together."

Her adoptive sisters stared at her blankly.

"Falling in love is like…" Kari's smile faltered. Her voice trailed off. "Actually I don't know what it feels like at all."

That realization stung more than she could have guessed it would. Having no attraction whatsoever to the men of this world, her last seventeen years of life on Galis had been loveless and sexless. She'd tried more times than she could count to relieve herself with a handsome servant, but the teary-eyed, emotionally fragile and coquettish ways of Galian men was like a proverbial bucket of ice water to the libido. As a result, her sex life consisted of imagination and masturbation. At least in her fantasies, men were *men*.

Klykka patted Kari on the hand. "Never fear, sister. When the desire to mate for life is upon you, we shall bag and tag the finest male specimen on Galis to make your own."

If only that knowledge made her feel better instead of worse. "Thank you," Kari managed. She forced a smile to her lips. "You're the best adoptive sisters a refugee from Earth could ask for."

"We should move on in topic," Klykka announced. "As interesting as your stories of primitive Earth are, I fear we have digressed from the subject at hand."

Kari blinked. "There was a subject at hand?"

"Aye. Your proficiency as a pack-hunter."

"Oh right."

"You have proved yourself an excellent hunter who can be bested by none. Leastways, there is no more need to apprentice under me any longer so — "

"You're making me leave?" Kari's heart sank and her stomach lurched. Klykka and Dorra were all she had. The thought of being forced to separate from them was equal parts terrifying and depressing.

"Nay!" Klykka retorted. "Child, I have instructed you more times than I can count not to interrupt my words with every musing that enters your mind. When will you learn?"

She was too relieved to be embarrassed by the admonishment. Thank the goddess, the holy sands, and everything else deemed sacred around here. Her silver-blue eyes shuttered as she blew out a breath. "My apologies, Mistress."

Klykka nodded, her contrition accepted. "Leastways, you require no more training in the art of hunting so 'tis time to train you in the art of warring."

Kari's eyes widened. The excitement she felt was no doubt obvious, but she tried to school her features anyway. Emotion was not acceptable *at all* when it came to warring; not even when the emotion in question was a positive one.

"'Tis a certainty you are permitted to show happiness for a moment," Dorra interjected. Her lips curled up. "Every rule has its exception."

When Klykka smiled too, Kari let herself grin. "I've been waiting for this day for seventeen Yessat Years! Thank you, Klykka!"

The Gy'at Li schooled her features. Dorra and Kari followed suit. "Before 'tis possible to learn the warring arts," the High Mystik explained, "one must learn the trade of their sector, and so you have."

Kari vigorously nodded, eager for her to move on and tell her more.

"One must also learn," Klykka said, "the erotic arts."

"I have. You trained me well." Kari gestured toward the erect penises of the five male servants The Gy'at Li had just purchased. "My spell has not worn off."

"For a certainty it has not, which is why I am confident 'tis time to test your skills on the males not of Galis."

Kari stilled. She hesitantly put a question to Klykka. "Males not of Galis?"

The High Mystik inclined her head. Her violet eyes narrowed, underscoring the seriousness of her command. "'Tis not permissible by Galian law to be taught the final steps in the warring arts until your Mistress is certain you can control males of all breeds by use of the erotic arts alone."

She wasn't certain what the connection between the erotic arts and the warring arts could possibly be, but Kari also implicitly understood that Klykka wouldn't tell her more than she wanted her to know until it was time.

"You will trek alone to the heart of Crystal City, child, and there you will live in the palace that belongs to me. For three moon-months you will work in the tavern frequented by male travelers from all over Trek Mi Q'an galaxy." Klykka leaned in closer to her. "Including the warriors of Tryston."

Kari suddenly felt thirsty. She held up her chalice so a male servant could refill it.

The warriors of Tryston? The ones who stole Galian females who were never heard from again?

"I would not send you did I not think you ready," Klykka said as if reading Kari's mind. The High Mystik smirked. "Leastways, the fool males will believe you to be naught more than a serving wench who puts on erotic shows for extra credits."

"Humanoids in general, but especially humanoid males, see what they expect to see," Dorra intoned. "'Tis not conceivable to their minds that tavern wenches are warriors in training, for in their worlds women serve no purpose but to pleasure men."

Kari frowned. Clearly Trek Mi Q'an, and Tryston in particular, were in need of some Gloria Steinems. Or some Galians.

She took a large sip of the *pici* juice her chalice had been replenished with as she marveled at the utter brilliance of Galian females. Not only were they training for war in plain sight, but the boot camp was being financed by the enemy.

"Heed my warning, sister," Klykka said sternly. "Perform for them, master your ability to control them, but do not ever—not under any circumstance—allow a Trystonni warrior to bed you."

Or face being kidnapped, possibly murdered, by the horrid males you've heard so many frightening stories about…

Klykka's meaning, unstated, was nevertheless understood. Kari slowly nodded. "I'm ready for the three moon-months to begin whenever you wish for me to go."

The Gy'at Li's expression was one of pride. Kari silently vowed to never disappoint her. "You will leave," Klykka pronounced, "on the morrow."

Chapter Six

Kari stepped into the teleport and out into Crystal City. When selling males on the marriage auction block, the Gy'at Lis had always teleported to the capital seat of Valor City where such dealings occurred and where foreigners were never granted access. But in the opulent Crystal City, where humanoids from every planet in Trek Mi Q'an galaxy were permitted to trade with Galians and do all the things tourists do was vastly different. It was, in a word, mesmerizing.

Kari couldn't help but to gawk at the soaring crystal structures that made the skyscrapers back on Earth look like huts by comparison. Try as she did, she couldn't see where the buildings ended. It was as if the shimmering towers rose past the moons and disappeared into the heavens. The sight was, without hesitation, the single most wondrous view she'd ever laid eyes on.

She walked down the main path into the metropolis as Klykka had instructed her to, but kept a slow pace so she could sightsee. Humanoid tradesmen of every color and size imaginable lined the street, hawking their wares. Children laughed together as they played, five young Galian boys holding hands and skipping like girls back on Earth would have done. Galian women strolled the bartering stalls with their eager-to-shop husbands, several of them buying trinkets for their men to ooh and aah over.

"Mistress, may I have it?" Kari overheard one husband squeal excitedly to his wife. "Am I worthy of the credits it might cost?"

"Aye, of course, my beloved," the wife responded. "You submit to me in all things and seek to please me at all times. 'Tis a boon you are worthy of."

Kari came to a sudden halt. This was the first time she'd ever seen what became of a Galian man after he was bagged and sold. She wasn't altogether certain what happened when a male was tagged, but clearly a deep bond was forged. She just wished it was a bond that didn't make her want to gag.

A thousand Yessat Years could tick by and a wimpy man like that would still fail to arouse her. That acknowledgment was more than a little depressing so she thrust it from her thoughts and resumed her open-mouthed marveling of the surroundings.

The decadence and sparkle of Crystal City had no rival. She was going to make the most of her three moon-months here and enjoy every *Nuba*-second of the experience. She smiled as she walked, excited by the prospects this new undertaking presented. Exploring Crystal City, if nothing else, would be an adventure unto itself.

She spotted a bartering stall where the most beautiful *zokas* she'd ever seen were on display. Kari picked up her pace, making a beeline straight for it. The gold *zokas* would make perfect gifts for Klykka and Dorra, while the sparkly one spun from black gemstones would look great on her. If nothing else, Kari thought, staring at it, the black *zoka* provided an interesting contrast against her porcelain skin— great for her upcoming performances on stage.

"You don the dress of a Galian warrior, but 'tis a certainty you haven't the look of our kind." The owner of the stall gave Kari the once-over. "Nor the height."

"I've been here seventeen Yessat Years, though. My Mistress sent me to Crystal City to wait tables and perform."

The Galian inclined her head. She implicitly understood the underlying implication. Namely that Kari was a warrior in training.

"You are *galishi*?"

Galishi—the Galian term for what amounted to a naturalized female citizen with full rights. The word was more meaningful than that though because it also denoted that Kari had been taken in by a High Mystik and raised as her own. "I am."

"From which sector?"

"Gy'at Li."

The owner looked impressed. "I herald from the Zha'Ri sector." She waved a hand toward the array of *zokas*. "'Tis an honor to trade with you. Purchase what you will."

"Thank you. I already know what I want though."

A minute later the three G-strings and their matching sandals were wrapped in a *vesha* pelt and handed over to her. Kari held up the palm of her hand so the Galian tradeswoman could laser-scan it, which would automatically transfer the credits from her account to the stall owner's.

"Next time." She waved the proffered credits away. "Tell your Mistress 'tis a gift from Nyoki whose allegiance is sworn to The Zha'Ri."

"I will. It was a pleasure to meet you, Nyoki. I am Kari."

"Likewise, Kari. Do you find yourself in need of aide, you have an ally in me and any warrior of the Zha'Ri sector."

Kari smiled. She inclined her head then resumed her stroll down the main path of the city centre. Lost in thought, she was too busy wondering over Nyoki's parting words to care about sightseeing. It wasn't so much *what* the Galian female had said as the manner in which she'd said it. Were there warriors in Crystal City from sectors hostile to The Gy'at Li? She would put the question to Klykka the next time they spoke.

A tingling sensation zinged through Kari's body as an odd feeling stole over her. Her senses instinctively kicked into hyper vigilance mode. Someone was watching her. No, *watching* was too weak a word for this feeling, she decided. The jolt of apprehension and awareness that was causing the hair at the nape of her neck to stand on end was what she expected a hunted animal felt like when trying to evade a large predator.

She came to a standstill and looked around. *"Always trust your instincts,"* she knew Klykka would instruct her if she were here. *"'Tis a gift from the goddess bestowed upon women, this is."*

Kari's gaze darted around, looking for the one who was causing the gift to kick in. Just when she was about to give up and resume walking, certain that her instincts had failed her and she was reacting in an overly sensitive manner because of her conversation with Nyoki, her silver-blue gaze honed in on a massive, muscled chest.

Holy. Shit.

Kari's breath caught in her throat. They were separated by the street, yet she was still forced to tilt her head back to look up at the largest giant of a man she'd ever before seen. His hair was black as the night, his skin and eyes as golden as finely aged whiskey. Standing nearly eight feet in height, his four hundred to five hundred pound frame was carved of solid, unyielding muscle. She swallowed roughly. This was no Galian male. Even had his eye color been violet, which it wasn't, his gaze was too commanding to belong to a male native to this planet.

He's a Trystonni warrior…

There went the gift again, telling her the one alien species of male she least wanted to interact with was watching her like a cheetah stalking a gazelle. Her gaze flew to his forehead where a skull had been tattooed into his skin, then down to the necklace he wore.

A Trystonni bridal necklace.

The gift hadn't lied. There was no question about it. She'd heard the stories of those necklaces, knew that if a Tryston warrior removed the one he wore and placed it around a woman's neck, she was bound to him forever — literally. The necklace made him able to track her should she flee and wouldn't unclasp until death, if even then.

Kari's breathing grew heavy, causing her breasts to heave and jiggle. The giant's gaze flicked down to study them. His eyes narrowed in arousal.

Kari's body responded against her volition, her pink nipples hardening and jutting out. Her heart rate picked up, causing her breathing to become impossibly more labored.

For seventeen Yessat Years she had worn the *zoka*; for more than sixteen of those years she'd grown so accustomed to near-nakedness in public that she no longer felt the vulnerability that went hand-in-hand with nudity back on Earth. Or at least she hadn't, Kari conceded, until this moment.

Standing in the heart of Crystal City, surrounded by more people than she'd ever before encountered, the silver *zoka* and turquoise sandals she wore provided no shield from the giant's covetous gaze. His golden eyes flicked back and forth between her painfully erect nipples and the G-string hiding her pussy from his view. The gift was screaming that he found the *zoka* a nuisance as it kept him from seeing what he most wanted to be inside of.

Kari blinked. She shook her head slightly, as if forcing herself to snap out of a sorcerer's spell.

Their gazes clashed again. The warlord's possessive, hungry eyes were at once arousing and frightening.

Kari dashed away, running as fast as her feet would carry her. She could feel the giant's gaze following her, branding her…

And promising her that they *would* meet again.

* * * * *

"This place is incredible." Kari stared in amazement at the penthouse she'd be calling home for the next three moon-months. "And the technology? Whoa!"

"Whoa? This is another one of your Earth words?"

"Yeah."

"'Tis not translating in my mind, that word."

"Because there's no Galian equivalent."

"I see."

Kari realized she was being rude. She forced herself to stop examining every inch of her new, temporary home so she could give The Gy'at Li's hologram her full attention. She plopped down on a purple crystal chair—then immediately shot back up to her feet. She gasped.

Klykka smiled. "You assumed a seat carved from crystal would feel hard and cold, aye?"

"Of course!" Kari frowned as she eyed the chair suspiciously. "But it felt like the softest *vesha* hide on the planet."

"'Twill not eat you, child," Klykka teased. "Be seated."

Kari hesitantly prepared to sit. She didn't really have a choice. An order was an order.

"For the love of the goddess," Dorra grunted, her hologram appearing next to Klykka's, "The Gy'at Li did not send you to Crystal City to kill you, sister. Leastways, she would have done so long before now did she not find your primitive reactions bemusing. Sit."

"*Primitive* reac— Now listen here, Dorra!"

"Remember the time you gave shelter to the visiting Tumians?" Dorra said to Klykka, effectively ignoring Kari. "'Twould have thought they were *heeka* beasts the way she screamed."

"Aye." The Gy'at Li grinned. She shook her head slightly. "'Twas a passing fair laugh she gave us."

Kari's nostrils flared. "I don't trust anything that has more than two legs," she gritted out.

"And the time she thought a *yoma* was trying to eat her?" Dorra continued. "The poor beast did naught but look at her."

"By the sands, aye!" Klykka said, chuckling. "I remember!"

Kari sat down on the chair. "Well maybe if you rode around in cars like normal Earthlings instead of on the backs of flying monkeys with huge fangs..." She folded her arms across her breasts. "And for the record," she huffed, "those Tumians are creepy, okay? They have eight fucking legs." She held up eight fingers to underscore her point. "Eight!"

"Wait until she spots a visiting *pugmuff* in Crystal City," Dorra mused. "Ahh—to be a holo-mirror on the wall when it happens."

"Can we move on?" Kari bit out. "For two women who rarely smile let alone belly laugh, you're sure making up for guffaws gone by."

"More of her Dearth words?" Dorra asked her sister.

"Aye."

"Earth!" Kari seethed. "They are Earth words!"

Dorra waved a dismissive hand. "Mayhap my most favored memory 'twas the moon-rising when she..."

Kari sighed, tuning her so-called sisters out. This had the makings of a long day. She grabbed a chalice from the table next to her. "Fuck the *pici* juice," she muttered under her breath, "I'm ready for the *matpow*."

"Oh aye, 'tis one of my favored memories as well! Leastways, 'tis almost as amusing as the eve when she…"

Kari stood and poured herself a drink. "To *matpow* and a raging buzz." She raised the chalice and toasted the air. Her lips smoothed into a grim line. "And to beating the shit out of my siblings."

* * * * *

"Have you familiarized yourself with the penthouse?" Klykka's hologram asked. "Need I explain aught else to you?"

"Oh I had plenty of time to look around while Dorra was here," Kari said drolly. "I'm sure I can manage."

Klykka hesitated. "You realize Dorra was not there, aye? Leastways, nor am I."

Kari slithered out of her *zoka*. "Yes, I realize that." She kicked off her sandals and sighed. "I won't pretend to understand how holograms and holo-images work, but my primitive mind grasps the fact you aren't actually here."

"Kari…"

"It's fine, Klykka. I'm fine. I just want to get some sleep."

"Kari, look at me."

She tried to school her features before obeying The Gy'at Li's command, but she'd never been much good at that.

"Your heart is in your eyes," Klykka murmured. Her violet gaze softened. "'Tis sorry I am your feelings are smarting. We should not have teased you thusly."

"Were you teasing?" Kari asked the question, but wasn't altogether certain she wanted the answer. "Or do you really only keep me around as your personal court jester?"

"Oh, child…" Klykka held out her hand. "I would that I could hold you right now. Alas, 'tis naught I can do but extend a hand that is not really there to you."

Kari blinked back tears. She blew out a breath. "That's the only part that hurt," she quietly admitted, "when Dorra said you haven't killed me only because I amuse you."

"Dorra loves you with all of her hearts, as do I, child." Her smile was at once reassuring and comforting. "Leastways, Dorra is as talented at making jests as you are at breaking bread with Tumians."

Kari snorted at that. "Point taken."

"I forget at times how young you still are. Mayhap because there are parts of you that are wizened. You are possessed of what you might have called an 'old soul' back on Earth."

"Thank you, Klykka." Kari inclined her head. "I needed to hear that."

"Take yourself to the *vesha* hides and rest. Your training begins on the morrow's moon-rising. Leastways, you will need your energy and wits about you at the tavern."

Kari raised an eyebrow. "To serve *matpow* and perform a show in the erotic arts? I might not be a High Mystik, but I'm pretty sure after all these years of training I can do that in my sleep."

"Nay, child. 'Tis not your ability I doubt. 'Tis my fear that visiting Trystonni warriors will attempt to lure you to their *vesha* hides. In a heightened state of arousal, 'tis a wicked powerful temptation to ignore."

"I saw one today." Kari's eyes rounded. "He was the biggest man I've ever seen." He was also the most primal, arousing, and handsome man she'd ever laid eyes on, but she decided not to mention that part. Klykka seemed worried enough. "They do not rape women, do they?"

Klykka waved that fear away. "Only weak, cowardly men rape women. Leastways, your training has made you too powerful an adversary for a male such as that."

She blew out a breath of relief. "Thank goodness for that."

"'Tis a rare beauty you are," Klykka said. "Most males—if not all males—shall covet you. Take to the *vesha* hides any humanoid of your choosing so long as they do not herald from Tryston."

Kari's cheeks pinkened. "You're saying that because you love me. I'm actually quite ordinary looking. What Trystonni would want me when thousands of females who look like *that* – " She waved her hand at Klykka. "Are walking around this city?"

"You seek to flatter me." Klykka grinned. "'Tis working."

Kari studied her adoptive sister from head to toe. The High Mystik was as naked as she was – no doubt heading to bed when the transmission ended – so it was easy to do. Everything about Klykka was Barbie doll perfect. From her long, silky black hair, to her violet eyes that glowed against the caramel coloring of her skin, to her perfect breasts, pouty lips, and bald pussy…

"I need not enter into lesser thought-lock with you to know where your mind is going." Klykka sighed. "On your Earth I might be extraordinary, but here I am quite ordinary."

"You're fucking perfect."

"And you've just become my favored sister." Klykka's smile, as brilliant as the rest of her, caused Kari to smile back. "Yet you are missing my point."

Kari's forehead wrinkled in thought. "You're saying that what is ordinary on Earth is extraordinary on Galis."

"Not just Galis, but all of Trek Mi Q'an. Mayhap even beyond."

That knowledge was as sobering as it was empowering. All her life she'd felt like the ugly duckling. The thought of Trystonni warriors finding her red hair and pale skin provocative was heady indeed. They were men further from ordinary than she'd believed possible. While she realized she couldn't have sex with one, just knowing they'd want to bumped her self-esteem up several necessary notches.

"Rest up, child. As I said, you'll need it."

"One last thing since I don't know when we'll talk next."

"Aye?"

"The woman I bought the *zokas* from..." Kari quickly recounted their conversation. "Am I being paranoid or—"

"Nay, you are not." Klykka frowned. "Leastways, no Galian warrior would dare to cross you so think no more upon it."

"Why not?"

"Because their sector would incur my wrath. 'Twould be my right under the holy law to wage war and no sector could withstand my assault."

Kari grinned, causing the dimples in her cheeks to pop out. "I knew you were a bad-ass, but I didn't know you were like *the* bad-ass."

Klykka winked. "Never forget it."

Later that night, alone in her bed, Kari's thoughts returned to the grim giant with golden eyes. The way he'd looked at her, the way her entire body had responded to his brazen stare…

Her hand slid down to her pussy. Her fingers found her clit and began rubbing.

She might not be allowed to fuck him, but she could damn sure fantasize about it.

Chapter Seven

Last night's orgasm must have knocked her out like a sedative because she slept in a hell of a lot later than she'd planned on. Kari had hoped to explore all the technological gadgets in the penthouse, not to mention take in some sightseeing, but she barely had time to figure how to shower and grab a bite to eat before she'd need to leave for the tavern.

Still quite groggy, Kari stepped into the bathing chamber and prepared to figure out how it worked. Standing in a conventional Galian room, she gasped when, a blink of an eye later, she found herself standing in a lushly green jungle under a cool, tropical waterfall. Macaws flew by, spider monkeys hunted for berries in the treetops...

Tears of happiness spilled from her eyes. She was home, back on Earth, drinking in the glorious Amazonian sun. The bathing chamber was somehow able to sense exactly what she needed and where she needed to be — the only thing missing was the sight of her sister.

Kari half-laughed and half-cried as she craned her neck and basked in the warmth. The waterfall's temperature and pressure was precisely what her body craved. She ran her fingers through her soaking wet hair and smiled up at the yellow sun she sorely missed. A cool breeze wafted past, hardening her nipples.

"I don't want to leave," she whispered. "I want to stay here forever."

Her brain knew this wasn't real, that either technology or magic was responsible for this earthly reunion, but neither did she care. She was *home*. And she was going to enjoy every moment of it.

The sounds of the rainforest were at once calming and stimulating, which Kari supposed was the point. The perfectly simulated environment felt so good, so reassuring, that she didn't care if she had time to eat before going to training — she wanted to stay exactly where she was for as long as she could. Unfortunately, nothing lasts forever.

A blink later and Kari was back in the ordinary bathing chamber, her hair dried and flawlessly styled, her body washed, exfoliated, dried, and polished. Even her mons had been trimmed and waxed into a perfect triangular patch.

"Why doesn't Klykka have one of these installed in her palace?" she muttered to the walls. She was already looking forward to her next shower. "This is too cool."

Five minutes later, Kari strolled out onto one of the penthouse's many terraces. Still naked, she sipped from a chalice of warm *jumya*, a beverage that was brewed from the blue leaves of *jumyun* trees. An array of fruits, breads, and the Galian version of cheese was spread out on the terrace's only table, ready for her to eat. She smiled. "It's going to be difficult to go back to the basics after living in the lap of luxury for three moon-months."

Why oh why did Klykka keep the palace so stark and simplified when she could obviously afford to live like a queen? Bathing chambers that sensed your needs, instantaneous food delivery at the click of a button, high-rise crystal structures with elevator-like machines that transported you in less than a heartbeat from the building's entrance to a luxurious penthouse 700 stories up...

This was the life. Indeed the only thing missing from it was a sexy, virile male to share it with.

That thought led to another, namely to the man she shouldn't be thinking about.

Plopping down on a *vesha*-soft crystal chair, Kari sighed as she set down her chalice of *jumya* and picked up a piece of fruit. Seventeen Yessat Years and the first male to arouse her was the one she couldn't have. Talk about bad fucking luck!

She bit into the fruit with the disgruntled force of a vampire who couldn't locate a good vein. Klykka had told her there would be humanoid males from all across Trek Mi Q'an galaxy in Crystal City. Kari hoped at least one of the various species looked like the warrior from Tryston she'd seen yesterday. She glanced poignantly toward the chalice of warm *jumya* and frowned.

Seventeen years. If she were a man, her balls would have been bluer than that fucking drink by now.

* * * * *

Nervousness set in as Kari walked into Mettle Tavern. The boisterous atmosphere should have been welcoming, but tonight, her first night on the job, it was unnerving. Wearing the black, sparkly *zoka* she'd purchased from Nyoki, her long, wine-red curls cascading past her butt, she looked pretty damn good if she did say so herself. Klykka must have been correct about Kari rating a perfect 10 on the exotic scale because every male who saw her walk past stared at her as though she were the sexiest woman alive.

It's about time, she sniffed, holding her head up high. Every woman deserved to feel like the belle of the ball at least once in her life. Apparently her turn had finally arrived. She conceded she'd probably enjoy her proverbial moment in the sun more if she didn't feel nervous enough to vomit on the customers.

"Kari Gy'at Li."

She came to a stop and looked around, unable to find the female voice that had called out her name. A group of Trystonni warriors were staring her down from the table they shared, their arousal obvious. Seated almost at floor level, they still looked taller than her while standing. She swallowed roughly, breaking eye contact.

Similar to a Japanese or Indian restaurant back home, the customers of Mettle Tavern sat on *vesha* pads that kept them close to the ground. The patrons shared their meals around tables that appeared to automatically adjust to the perfect height for every group. Humanoids and non-humanoids — holy shit did that thing have an ass for a head?! — interacted, but mostly sat or lounged with members of the same species.

"Kari Gy'at Li."

Kari crooked her neck. The voice was distinctly feminine, yet the only females in the tavern were the ones serving food and drink to the clients. For some enigmatic reason it gave her a thrill to know those women were warriors in training, yet the visiting males believed them to be, in their eyes at least, "lowly" serving wenches.

That's right, misogynists, she thought on her second haughty sniff of the night, score one for the home team.

"Kari Gy'at Li."

At last Kari spotted her. The gorgeous Galian female making her way toward Kari had to be Arista, the warrior who owned Mettle Tavern. Klykka had instructed her that Arista would know who she was when she walked through the doors.

"I see The Gy'at Li did not exaggerate your beauty," Arista purred in Trystonni. Kari knew the table of warriors from Tryston were listening, which embarrassed her a bit. Coming to a halt in front of her, the female warrior ran a hand through her hair. "Fire-berry indeed. Leastways, this explains your name."

Kari. The Galian word for fire-berry.

"Yes, Mistress," she returned in Galian, hoping the warriors didn't speak their tongue. "My hair is unusual for Trek Mi Q'an." She smiled, her dimples popping out. "Or so I'm always told."

"And you have a small patch of fire-berry above your mons?"

The warriors made appreciative murmurs, indicating they spoke Galian just fine. Shit. How mortifying.

"I do," Kari stated, hoping the heat she felt on her face wasn't showing.

"I am Arista."

"I know."

Her smile was slow and sensual. Kari hoped that meant she was being accepted as an apprentice. She knew protocol dictated that she say nothing until spoken to—at least not until Arista decided to take her under her wing.

The seasoned warrior Klykka had praised as the best teacher of the erotic arts in Galis took her time visually inspecting Kari. Her violet gaze raked all over her body, making her aware of her near nakedness. She managed to remain stoic despite the earthly instinct to shrivel into the shadows. She just hoped the teacher accepted her so no shame was brought to the House of Gy'at Li.

After what felt like forever, Arista resumed eye contact. Inclining her head, for the average Galian woman stood several inches taller than her, the tavern's owner gently cradled Kari's face and began to kiss her. Kari could sense the Trystonni warriors' arousal. They obviously thought this was an erotic show, but Kari knew what it meant.

Arista thrust her tongue inside Kari's mouth, her hands falling to tweak her nipples. Kari moaned and wrapped her arms around the Galian's neck, kissing her back with everything she had to give, excited and grateful Arista had accepted her as an apprentice.

To outsiders, this was a show of sexuality. To Galians, the meaning was dependent on the situation. Regardless of the condition, the physical joining allowed Galians to link with each other in *fatoomi*—or fearlessness—a lesser form of thought-lock.

Kari's mind merged with Arista's in the void she'd learned long ago to not resist. It permitted them to have conversations nobody could eavesdrop in on.

"I accept you as mine, Kari Gy'at Li."

"Thank you, Mistress."

"You will retain the name of your sector, though you belong to the House of de Valor whilst under my dominion."

"The House of de Valor?" Arista was from the royal line itself! "I am not worthy."

"Aye, you are. If my finest, strongest warrior sends you to me, you are worthy."

Kari's eyes widened. "I did not mean disrespect to Klykka, my adoptive sister. My love and respect for her is—"

"I know, child." Arista smiled. "'Tis 750 Yessat Years since the day I was birthed. There is little I don't know."

Kari nodded, but said nothing.

"When we break fatoomi you will follow me without words into my private chambers. There we shall discuss your next three moon-months."

"Yes, Mistress."

"I give you leave to speak to me at your will."

"Thank you, Mistress."

Arista broke the kiss and the *fatoomi* came to an end. The Trystonni warriors looked ready to come, assuming they already hadn't. Either oblivious or unimpressed, Arista paid them no attention. She turned on her heel and strode away. Kari cleared her throat, quickly broke eye contact with the male warriors, and obediently followed behind her.

* * * * *

Arista's private chambers were also on the 700th floor. She dwelled in the soaring white crystal tower behind the tavern instead of the purple one in front of it where Kari lived. Just like Klykka's palace, Arista de Valor's mansion was technologically advanced and opulent in its splendor. Kari followed closely behind her. When they passed the bedchamber doors, she couldn't help but notice the twenty to thirty males of Arista's harem lounging around inside it, penises fully erect, waiting for their Mistress's attention.

"You fear that a Galian male will never please you," Arista said without looking back, startling Kari. She continued walking toward what appeared to be the palace's dining hall. "Leastways, 'tis naught to worry about, child."

Kari's mouth worked up and down, but it took a protracted moment to get her question out. "How did you know?"

Arista didn't respond until they reached the great hall. She motioned for Kari to be seated at the table.

"There are fewer older than I in Trek Mi Q'an, child. Mayhap only the Chief Priestess of Tryston herself has seen more moon-risings."

Ari. Klykka had told her a little about the Chief Priestess, but not much. "Isn't Ari like a thousand Yessat Years old?"

"Mayhap more. Leastways, none can say." Arista took a seat directly across from Kari at the dining table. "Ari was birthed from the belly of the goddess, yet she is half-mortal."

Kari thought back on her history lessons. "Her father was a Trystonni warrior chosen by the goddess Aparna." Her nose crinkled. "Correct?"

"Aye."

"Her father died?"

"He breached the Rah the moment his seed took root."

According to the dominant religion of the galaxy, the Rah was like a gate that separated the world of mortals from those who'd passed on into immortality. "He died the moment the goddess became impregnated?"

"Though 'tis natural to grieve a loved one who has breached the Rah, for a certainty no soul ever truly dies, child. Ari was born on the other side of the Rah, and because she is half-divine she has the power to visit there at will." Arista pressed a button and beverages instantaneously appeared. "Ari herself told me our loved ones await us in paradise and so it is."

Apparently religion was the same everywhere. It provided what those in mourning most needed — hope.

"Do not dismiss these lessons as fanciful thoughts, child. Leastways, it matters naught do you believe for what is will always be."

Kara looked to the table. "But that means I'll never see my sister again."

"Nay. It means quite the opposite."

Her head shot up. She searched Arista's gaze. "But religion where I come from is different."

"Klykka tells me your people worship the male one-god."

"Yes."

Arista shrugged. "'Twill mayhap be a surprise to them when they breach the Rah, yet for a certainty the goddess will not turn them away."

For some reason her explanation not only made sense, it also made Kari feel better. She'd resisted religious teachings and texts since her arrival on Galis, afraid to contemplate what believing in them could mean, only to discover her greatest comfort was to be found in that which she'd most feared. Ignorance, she supposed, wasn't the bliss it's credited to be.

"It never is, child."

Kari's eyes rounded. "You can read my mind?"

"Nay. Leastways not until you are a High Mystik able to enter into *hyatzi*, the highest and most powerful form of thought-lock."

"Dorra isn't a High Mystik, yet I've heard Klykka say they've entered into *hyatzi* together."

"Aye, but 'tis one-sided, child. Klykka can reach *hyatzi* without Dorra, but Dorra cannot reach it without her sister or another High Mystik. Leastways, you see the difference."

"Like the day Klykka found me and pulled me into the silver waters with her?"

"Aye."

"Why did Dorra never train to become a High Mystik?"

Arista shrugged. "'Tis not within the power of every warrior, child. Were we all of us High Mystiks in the making, there would be none to take orders."

Kari couldn't stop herself from laughing. "You got me there."

Arista smiled, her full lips curving. "In answer to your question, nay, I cannot read your mind."

"Then...?"

"A child cannot school their emotions, though they always believe themselves capable."

Kari sighed. "In my world, I'm not a child. I'm a middle-aged woman."

"Be grateful you are *galishi* then."

She grinned. Point taken.

Hesitant to ask the question foremost on her mind, she was relieved when Arista answered it for her. "You find naught appealing of Galian males."

"No." Kari sighed a breath of relief, grateful to be able to unburden herself. "They are handsome, of course, but their mannerisms and emotionalism cancel out and overpower their good looks for me."

Arista's look was thoughtful as she poured herself a chalice of warm, blue *jumya*. She was silent for a long moment as she sipped from the cup. When she placed the chalice back on the table, her gaze found Kari's. "'Tis not often we make war on others, but when 'tis necessary those we conquer become our chattel under the holy law. Leastways, not all Galian husbands are born here. Some of them are sold into matrimony, yet they are who they are. For a certainty they possess the fierceness and mettle you so crave. Would you care for a drink?"

Kari blinked at the turn in subject.

"I've *jumya*, *pici*, and *matpow* to offer. What is your desire, child?"

With this conversation? There wasn't a contest. "I'll take the *matpow*. I have a feeling I'm going to need it."

Arista's smile was equal parts devilish and angelic. "Aye. You will."

The conversation with Arista de Valor lasted for three hours. The High Mystik freely answered every question Kari put to her then sent her home for the remainder of the night. She wanted Kari to process her thoughts and prepare for the next evening when she officially commenced her training.

Kari was grateful for the reprieve because her brain truly did need time to absorb all she'd learned. Waiting tables and performing an erotic show would have been too much after the tête-à-tête she'd engaged in with Arista.

Exiting Mettle Tavern and walking toward the crystal tower she called home, Kari was too distracted to notice much of anything, including the glowing golden gaze that tracked her every move. The prey wasn't aware of the predator's stare, but the hunter knew he'd successfully located the hunted.

Chapter Eight

Kari stared at herself in the holo-mirror as she tried to calm her nerves. Arista had instructed her to enter Mettle Tavern through the back doors guarded by female warriors, rather than through the front ones guarded by no one. She was grateful for that option because she was able to enter her private dressing room without being bothered by customers.

Dressing room. She mentally harrumphed at the misnomer. A more appropriate term would be *un*dressing room because she'd be working totally in the nude. Worse, nude and oiled down.

When she'd arrived in Crystal City it was under the impression that all the women who worked in Mettle Tavern were warriors-in-training. That turned out not to be the case. "I've changed the way I do things since Klykka trained under me," Arista had told her. "Leastways, 'twas two hundred years ago, that. You need serve trenchers of food only whilst one of the servers is absent or the tavern has more patrons than anticipated. At those times, we all pitch in."

In essence most of the serving wenches were in fact serving wenches. They were warriors, yes, but they would never be High Mystiks. It was the performers who were apprenticing under The de Valor. Arista had decided a long time ago that lesser warriors who heralded from sectors that specialized in serving were needed to wait tables full-time so the warriors-in-training could focus on the mind-and-body control techniques employed in the erotic arts. The techniques, so crucial, were the same as those used in battle, though to different ends.

Almost time for my first performance...

She was thinking too much, which increased her anxiety exponentially. Her heart was racing and her breathing was too rapid. She needed to calm down.

A holo-image zapped into the mirror. It was Klykka.

"I don't think I can do this," Kari said on a gasp. "I'm literally shaking!"

Klykka's expression was kind, but firm. "Aye you can. Leastways, I would not have sent you otherwise."

"Remember all the sexual hang-ups I had when I first came to Galis?"

"Aye."

"They're back," Kari panted. "I think for good this time."

Klykka's laugh was somewhat comforting. It also made her realize what a chicken shit she was being. "'Tis nerves, this, and naught more."

But still…

"Klykka—"

"You can and you will finish your training, Kari Gy'at Li. 'Tis three bedamned moon-months you have to master your powers, yet for a certainty 'tis doubtful you'll need more than a sennight." She shrugged. "Your time in Crystal City 'tis no more than a formality."

Kari bit her lip.

"'Tis a vow betwixt sisters, Kari," The Gy'at Li said softly. "You are ready and you can do this."

Kari blew out a breath. She obediently inclined her head. "I'm sorry. I guess I am a little nervous."

"And so you should be. 'Tis the first time you will attempt to command an entire chamber filled with males not of our species. I would worry did you not feel fear."

As always, the High Mystik knew exactly what to say to calm her down. And yet…

"What if I suck? What if I can't command the entire tavern tonight? What if Arista sends me away?"

"I've yet to meet any warrior-in-training who commanded the entire chamber on her first attempt." Klykka waved that away. "Leastways, relax and enjoy yourself. The more at ease you are with your sexuality, the more provocative you will be."

A glowing, pulsating light blinked twice—Kari's cue that she was due to perform in five *Nuba*-minutes. Her heart was beating so fast she felt faint.

"Go," The Gy'at Li commanded. "All will be well." With those final words, Klykka's holo-image vanished.

An idea struck Kari, one she hadn't thought of before. Slipping into her black *zoka* and grabbing her matching sandals, she left her dressing room and walked toward the stage.

"What are you doing, child?" Arista whispered in a harsh voice. "Remove the *zoka* and—"

"Trust me." Kari pleaded with her through wide, silver-blue eyes. "Please."

Arista frowned. "I've no bedamned time to debate this so apparently I must!" She didn't look pleased, but she exited onto the stage.

Still behind the stage where customers couldn't view her, Kari closed her eyes and steadied her breathing. She entered into the trance-like state it had taken years of training to reach.

She could hear Arista announcing her arrival to the gathered throng, but the meditative state kept her calm.

Kari's private parts were covered, but she would be nude before the performance ended. Arista might not have understood why, but some niggling feeling told Kari none of the patrons had ever seen a striptease before. She just hoped to hell and back that Arista would be proud of her initiative.

Since *zokas* didn't have a top portion, she had made do by ripping off the scarf-like strings from her sandals and quickly fashioning them into something of a bra. With naturally large breasts, the black strips of cloth covered only her nipples and tied behind her back.

"'Tis with great pleasure," Arista's voice boomed out, "that I introduce to you the most seductive and beautiful apprentice ever known to me..."

Kari's eyes flew open. She grunted. Even if The de Valor was only saying that to get the crowd riled up, it was a lot of fucking pressure! Praise the goddess for trances. And *matpow*.

"From the House of Gy'at Li, under the protection of her sister and Mistress, I give to you..."

Just say my name already! I feel like a slutty boxer being publicized by the Don King de Valor!

"Kari..."

Primitives can out-sexy anyone. I've got this! Fuck! Shit! Fuck!

"Gy'at…"

Hurry up!

"Liiiiiiiiiiii!"

I very well may faint!

The crowd burst into raucous applause the same moment the music cued. Their excitement was palpable and bolstered her confidence—at least enough to give her the courage to walk on stage.

The shimmering lights dimmed and the spotlight basked her in a fiery glow. The tavern fell silent. She smiled inwardly, knowing she'd made the right bet—they had no idea what a striptease was. Primitive Earthlings: 1, The Allegedly Advanced: 0.

The music was simultaneously hypnotic and sensual. Kari sauntered toward middle stage, strolling like a fashion model on the catwalk in slow motion. All eyes were on her, waiting to understand what came next. She could see Arista standing backstage gnawing at her lip.

Kari looked to the crowd, a sensual smile curving her lips. She raised her hands above her head before slowly bringing them down to rest above her breasts. Trailing her hands down to the strip of cloth covering her nipples, she started to remove it, showing a hint of her areolas, then put the cloth back.

The crowd roared. She could feel Arista's approval without looking toward her to confirm it.

Turning around to give the crowd her back, she threw the patrons a naughty look from over her shoulder while playing with the ties that held the cloth together. Again, the customers cheered. She undid the tie and let it fall away while keeping her breasts shielded from view by holding the cloth in place. The hollering grew louder.

Methodically and sensuously turning to face the crowd, she held the strip across her nipples, her breasts spilling out both over and under it. The men wanted to see her nipples more than they wanted air to breathe. She gave her breasts a jiggle, teasing the patrons, and earning louder cheers than before. Biting her lip in a playful manner, she used the cloth like a feather boa, slithering it around, but not letting it fall.

It was all they could take; the crowd went wild.

Kari prepared to drop the cloth. Deciding to make eye contact with one of the customers, she zeroed in on the man closest to her. Her eyes widened. She did a double-take. Kari's breath caught in the back of her throat as her silver-blue gaze clashed with a glowing gold one too familiar and commanding to ignore. It was *him*.

Out of all the taverns in Crystal City, the Trystonni warrior of her most fevered fantasies had managed to track her down. She didn't know how she knew he'd hunted her in particular, but she did. His eyes, heavy-lidded with arousal, narrowed in on the nipples he badly desired to see. He wanted to do more than look, she realized, but looking was all he would get.

His arousal empowered her. The fierce warrior had managed to throw her off her game for a *Nuba*-second, but Kari was back in control. She let the cloth fall to the ground, her puffy, pink nipples bared and erect, her wine-red curls cascading down her shoulders and framing her body. She could hear the patrons shouting and hooting, but her attention was focused solely on the only man she'd wanted in seventeen years—the one she couldn't allow herself to have.

She played with her nipples, tweaking and massaging them, her gaze not straying from his. His erection was visible through the black leather pants all males of his species wore. His golden gaze, so possessive, stayed trained on her nipples. She knew he wanted to suck them and that knowledge was the most powerful aphrodisiac in all the worlds combined.

Next was the *zoka*. She teased and taunted, gave the audience her back again, and pretended to remove it. When the crowd groaned, she didn't care, for it was only *his* reaction that mattered. Sliding the *zoka* down so he could see her bare ass, Kari bent over and gave him an unobstructed view of her wet pussy. She heard him mutter something imperceptible under his breath. He reached out to touch her cunt, but she stood up and pulled her thong back on. The tavern roared.

Turning again to face the warrior, this time Kari slid out of the *zoka* and let it fall to the floor. She could hear the shouting, but it didn't signify. Again, *he* was all that mattered.

His golden gaze zeroed in on her triangular patch of wine-red hair. She let him run his fingers through it, didn't resist when he rubbed her clit, and allowed herself to reenter the trance.

She sat in front of the giant, legs spread wide open, and massaged her pussy for his viewing pleasure. Allowing herself to go deeper into the trance, Kari's mind reached the void — the source of all power. Too aroused to feel the elation she deserved to feel for reaching it, she used her power from within the void to bring the audience into an arousal-lock. From this moment until she broke the trance, the customers would feel everything she did.

Kari played with her nipples, plumping them up, and moaning from the pleasure. The patrons followed suit, all of them experiencing the very hedonism Kari was. Her gaze found the warlord's. His breathing, in tune with hers, was heavy with arousal.

Like a wild animal unable to control himself, the warrior buried his face between her thighs and sucked on her pussy as if he owned it. Kari groaned as her head lolled back. The crowd groaned in response, unable to break her spell if they'd wanted to. The giant's callused hands found her breasts. His fingers massaged her stiff nipples. Kari's breathing grew increasingly labored as the warlord sucked harder, his possessiveness a tangible feeling.

Her orgasm was explosive. She knew from the moaning and shouts of satisfaction permeating the air that the audience was coming as hard as she was. She could feel the warrior's hot cum spurt from his cock as though it was inside her. He kept sucking on her cunt as he came, forcing a second, harder orgasm on her.

Kari screamed from the intensity of it. The patrons came so hard that all but one of them passed out. That one kept nuzzling her pussy, his tongue curling around her clit and demanding more. She gave him what he wanted, her fingers running through his hair while pressing his face closer. "I'm coming!" she wailed. "Only for you — *ohhhhh!*"

The mutual orgasm was so strong, so all-consuming, that Kari damn near passed out from it too. The giant at last lifted his face from between her thighs. His breathing was heavy and perspiration slicked his skin as his golden gaze found hers. He knew he was losing consciousness and that she would be able to run away. The last look he gave her before succumbing to blackness promised her that she could run, but he'd always find her.

Kari broke the trance. Taken off guard by the powerful connection she felt to the unconscious warrior, she shakily stood up. Her eyes wild, she looked at Arista. The de Valor inclined her head, proud. Kari nodded her gratitude and fled back to the crystal penthouse.

Chapter Nine

"You commanded the entire audience on your first attempt?" Dorra's hologram asked. She looked bewildered and in awe. "For a certainty?"

Kari's chin notched up. "I sure did."

"She is the first to ever accomplish a feat such as this," Klykka's hologram proudly announced. "'Tis honor you have brought to the House of Gy'at Li, Kari. My hearts are swollen with pride."

"As are mine," Dorra chimed in. "Leastways, you are the talk of the entire sector. My'ani is set to give birth any day now. She wishes to name the babe for you should the goddess gift her with a girl-child."

"Are you serious?" Kari enthused. "Wow!"

Recalling the last movie she'd seen on Earth mere months before her departure, Kari allowed herself to relish in the glory that came from being Neo—*The One!*—for a moment. She had mastered her own matrix, albeit a pervy one. In fact, Arista said after she taught her a few more mind-and-body control techniques, her apprenticeship would be over. That gave her almost three moon-months in Crystal City to spend her time as she pleased.

Kari felt like she'd conquered Mount Everest, won Olympic gold—or graduated as the valedictorian from Sodom and Gomorrah High. However one chose to view it, it was a job well done.

"Will you be returning home early?" Dorra asked.

"'Tis unlikely," Klykka wryly interjected. "Leastways, she has earned the right to holiday for a spell."

"Were I you, I would sample every cock that crossed my path," Dorra said matter-of-factly.

Kari grinned. "I'm hoping to sample something." Unfortunately, the cock she wanted so badly belonged to a man she couldn't tempt fate with by trying. She decided against mentioning that part. "I also told Arista that as long as I'm in Crystal City I'll be glad to serve tables on the nights she needs additional help."

"'Tis a generous boon, that." Klykka inclined her head. "You make us proud. Now get yourself some sleep. You look nigh unto exhausted."

"I am."

"Dorra and I leave for a pack hunt on the morrow so you shan't hear from us again. Leastways, not until our return."

Kari nodded. Her smile was sleepy. "Good hunting."

* * * * *

The next week was the busiest period in Kari's life. Her days were filled with Arista's training, her nights with erotic performances, and her stint at Mettle Tavern was nearing its end. Other than occasionally waiting tables when—and if—the need arose, her time would officially become her own after tomorrow night's performance. She had been taught well and learned eagerly. She had surpassed Arista's expectations and earned her respect. She should have been happy, should have been ecstatic in fact, but she wasn't. As much as she hated admitting it, she knew the reason why.

It was *him*. The giant, brooding warrior with the glowing, gold gaze and a skull tattooed into his forehead. The muscled warlord whose name she didn't even know.

He hadn't returned to Mettle Tavern since her premiere performance. Kari had expected to fend him off every night, doing her damnedest to thwart his advances, but such was not the case. Her pride wasn't smarting, which left her with one unmistakable and utterly frightening conclusion:

She missed him.

She didn't know him and could never attempt to try so thinking about him was pointless, yet the weirdly inexplicable connection she felt toward him was all-consuming. Stranger still, she knew — *knew* — he felt it too.

Plopping into bed, Kari let out a sigh and absently stared at the ceiling. He was her every daytime thought and her every nighttime fantasy. He was everything she wanted in a man and all she couldn't have. And he was throwing her off her game without even knowing it.

Earlier this evening she had helped out by serving trenchers of food and drink to the patrons overflowing the tavern. Kari had been so distracted by thoughts of the colossal warrior that when two vacationing females asked her what her name was, she had said "Kara" without thinking. She'd quickly corrected herself and told them she hadn't gone by that name in years and was now called Kari.

There had been something eerily familiar about one of those women, but by the time it dawned on her what that something was, the traveler was nowhere to be found. The female had looked...*earthy*. Weirder still, she had the height and accent of a woman who heralded from her home planet. Her speech pattern was what one would expect from a human who'd been whisked away from Earth in the 1960s.

The moment Kari's hazy mind cleared enough to question her had turned out to be a heartbeat too late. She'd asked one of the serving wenches about the foreign woman only to be told she'd fallen ill and had been removed from Mettle Tavern by the warlord Kil Q'an Tal, the brother of the emperor and king of Tryston's dominant red moon Morak. "Leastways, she was mayhap a bound servant who fled from her Master," the serving wench had informed Kari. "He likely came to collect her and return her to his harem."

Kari had swallowed rather roughly after hearing that, the reality of what Trystonni warriors do to women they snare fortified in her consciousness. That reinforcement alone should have made her overjoyed that the giant hadn't returned for her, yet it didn't.

"I'm going crazy," Kari whispered aloud. She closed her eyes and prayed for sleep. "Let him go," she instructed herself, "just let him go."

* * * * *

"'Tis honored I am to have trained you, Kari Gy'at Li." Arista de Valor's smile was infectious. "Leastways, what little training you needed! By the sands, Klykka taught you well."

"Thank you, Arista. That means a lot coming from you. I'm certain Klykka will feel the same way." Kari nostalgically scanned her now former dressing room. "I'm actually going to miss this place." Her silver-blue gaze returned to the The de Valor. She absently cast a glance over the High Mystik's ever-perfect form. Arista always looked stunning and tonight was no exception. The golden *zoka* and violet sandals she wore accented her caramel coloring while drawing attention to her almond-shaped, indigo eyes. "But I'll especially miss you."

"None of that, child." Arista embraced her with the warmth, pride, and bittersweet sentiment of a mother telling her daughter goodbye just before the teenager left home for university. "For a certainty you may visit me whenever you so desire. And do you ever need me? You now understand how to pull me into *hyatzi*."

Kari blew out a breath. "Let's hope the need for thought-lock never arises."

"War is coming to Trek Mi Q'an, child. Mayhap not for many moon-risings, but 'twould be naïve to think we will never again see battle."

"Do you really believe we could withstand an attack by Tryston?"

"If it came to that, aye, I do. And after you complete the final, necessary step of your training in the warring arts, you will believe it too."

"They're so big," Kari murmured. "And ruthless."

"Yet they know naught of Galis beyond the taverns and bartering stalls. Our technology, our training, even the vast majority of our terrain...it all remains a mystery to them." Arista smiled as she released Kari from her embrace. "Do not waste your moon-risings fearing the unlikely, child. The emperor has no reason to attack us."

Kari blinked. One wine-red eyebrow rose. "Then what do you mean about war coming to Trek Mi Q'an?"

Arista's expression was contemplative. "I cannot say as I do not know. 'Tis naught but a feeling I have, this." Arista sighed. "Ancient I may be, but Ari I am not. Only She Who is Borne of the Goddess can foretell destiny."

"But this feeling..." Kari tried to understand. "You don't believe it has to do with Tryston and Galis going to war?"

"Nay. If anything we will be allies, just as we were when the insurrectionists of Tron wreaked their havoc across the galaxy."

"So the war coming to Trek Mi Q'an will be started by those not from it?"

Arista was silent for a protracted moment. "'Tis the gift of intuition bestowed upon females coupled with the wisdom of an ancient that gives me...well, 'tis difficult to describe, but one might call it a knowing. Not a seeing as Ari experiences, just a knowing."

That was plenty of proof for Kari. Arista was never wrong. "This knowing tells you war is coming?"

"A darkness has breached Trek Mi Q'an." The de Valor inclined her head. "Aye. 'Tis the knowing that tells me war will be made against it."

Kari visibly shivered.

"None of that, child." Arista smiled before embracing her a final time. "You've two and a half moon-months of leisure to experience. Go enjoy it."

* * * * *

Kari returned to the *zoka* bartering stall she'd first visited upon her arrival in Crystal City. She wanted to have a few more *zokas* made for her sisters and herself. Nyoki Zha'Ri was eager to oblige. Apparently very few patrons ordered custom-made *zokas* because Nyoki seemed excited by the artistic challenge.

"I love the maroon one I'm wearing," Kari said. "It was purchased for me as a gift by The Gy'at Li." She whirled around to show the tradeswoman every angle. "I'm hoping you can make a similar one that matches my hair a bit closer."

"The color of the fire-berry?" Nyoki's chin notched up. "I can spin the jewels to be an exact match."

"Really?"

"'Tis a vow amongst Galians."

"How long will it take?"

"The gemstones I require must be bartered from one of the far sectors before it can be spun." She pursed her lips in thought. "'Mayhap one moon-month? Leastways, two at most."

"I'm not sure how much longer I'll be in Crystal City. If I pay extra credits can you send it by *yoma* when it's finished?"

Nyoki waved a hand. "I have never charged a customer more credits for delivery do they dwell within Galis. For a certainty I shan't start now." She grinned. "'Tis true then that The Gy'at Lis still rely upon the *yoma* for travel and deliveries?"

"Klykka insists on keeping everything as utilitarian and basic as possible. She doesn't believe warriors should ever rely on technology so very little in our sector is based on it." Kari grinned back. "So yeah, we still use the flying monkeys."

"There's no method of instant transport available in your sector?"

"We have holo-ports for humanoids coming to and going from our sector, but no transporters once you're inside. From there it's all done by *yoma*."

"I may just deliver the *zokas* myself. In all my moon-risings I've yet to see a *yoma* in person."

"They are much bigger standing next to you than they look in the sky."

"Now I know 'twill be I who makes the delivery. I needs must see this!"

They chatted for a few more minutes after which Kari paid the necessary credits for her purchases. "It's been a pleasure, Nyoki." Kari smiled. "If I don't see you again before I leave Crystal City then I hope to see you in my sector."

"You will, *galishi*. 'Tis a vow, that."

Kari admired Klykka more after her conversation with Nyoki Zha'Ri than she had before, which was saying a lot. She'd never understood her adoptive sister's insistence on retaining such Spartan ways, but she got it now. Klykka was actually quite genius. If Galis ever came under attack, the Gy'at Li sector would be the toughest to breach let alone conquer. Technology couldn't be used against them, making the *yoma* the only available transportation system. More loyal than dogs to their humans, the flying monkeys of Gy'at Li would defend their humanoids to the death.

Kari strolled back toward the purple, crystal dwelling that was her temporary abode. Lost in thought, she didn't realize she was being tracked.

Or that the one hunting her could barely contain his fury.

Chapter Ten

Kari walked into the nearest entrance pod of the purple, crystal edifice. The doors to the pod whisked shut behind her. She held up her palm so the transporter could identify her and instantaneously spit her out on the 700th floor. Stepping out of the transport, she heard the pod whizz shut.

"You permitted another warrior to touch you."

Kari yelped. Her eyes round and heart racing, she whirled around to face the intruder.

Her breath caught in the back of her throat. It was *him*. He hadn't forgotten her after all. Half elated to see him and half wary about his presence in Klykka's penthouse, she latched onto the latter. "How did you get in here?"

"Why did you permit another warrior to taste you?"

"I asked you a question."

"Why?" he barked.

Kari's nose wrinkled. "I don't know what you're talking about."

His golden gaze was frightening in its intensity. His musculature, intimidating on a normal day, was increasingly so tonight. She could see his vein-roped arms cording and tensing, which only served to exaggerate her wariness. He looked ready to kill her where she stood. Swallowing roughly, Kari instinctively took a step back.

"You permitted another warrior to lick your channel."

She blinked. "My channel?"

"Aye. Your channel."

She ran a shaky hand through her hair. "I don't even know what a channel is and you never answered my question." She forced her chin up and feigned a sense of control over the situation she didn't feel. "Until you answer it, I'm done listening to this."

"I have my ways," the giant murmured. "Leastways, you paid no heed to your surroundings when trekking back from the bartering stalls. 'Twas not difficult to enter the transport behind you."

How did a man so large walk so quietly? There she went swallowing again.

For some reason, until this moment, Kari hadn't noticed all his tattoos. There was more than the skull on his forehead — his chiseled arms were covered in them. The effect would have been arousing under normal conditions, but in this circumstance it only added further intimidation to his already commanding presence.

"A channel," the warrior grimly instructed Kari, "is what Galians call a pussy." He took a single step, putting him directly in front of her. "For a certainty you let another warrior touch and lick upon it."

Kari's mouth worked up and down, but nothing came out.

"Never lie to me, *pani*."

Pani. The Trystonni word for "baby" that differed in meaning upon its context. Since she wasn't his child, Kari safely assumed he'd just called her by an intimate term of endearment. *Channel* must have been Trystonni slang for she'd never heard the word before, but *pani* she definitely knew. She didn't know whether to feel honored or terrified.

"You mean during one of my last shows?"

"Aye."

She flung her arm out. "You weren't there and I had a job to do!" She took another step back so she could glare up at his face. Her eyes narrowed. "I looked for you. Every night I looked! Finally Arista started getting suspicious and asked why I hadn't let another patron bring me to peak." Her lips turned down. "I did what I had to do."

His glowing, gold gaze searched her silvery-blue one. "You looked for me?"

Kari's face blanched. She shouldn't be encouraging him. She knew what his kind did to women. She broke his stare and cast her eyes downward.

"You looked for me?" His hand, massive enough to crush her skull like a tin can, cradled her chin and gently prodded it up. "Answer me," he murmured.

"Yes," she quietly admitted, "I did."

His gaze searched hers. She wanted him so bad she could cry.

"You should go." Kari pulled away and walked toward the doors, preparing to press the button that would summon the pod. She had to remain strong and keep her promise to Klykka. "This can't happen. This can *never* happen."

He didn't move, just watched her. "I can smell your arousal, wee one."

Kari blew out a breath. She didn't know if he meant that literally, but suspected he did. Either way, his thickly murmured words made her arousal a thousand times worse.

"I don't even know your name," Kari said feebly. She regained her self-control long enough to wave a dismissive hand. "Not that it matters because *this* can't happen!"

"It can. And for a certainty, it will."

Her eyes widened. "You mean to rape me?"

"I won't have to rape you."

She wished her mouth wasn't cotton-dry because the need to gulp yet again was paramount. "This," she shakily repeated, "can never happen." She steeled herself against any argument the warlord might make. She raised a palm. "I know what your kind do to women and it won't be done to me. You need to leave. *Please*."

"What do we do?" he asked. His expression was stoic, but his eyes were amused.

Her jaw tightened. "You steal women. You put those weird necklaces around their necks—" She pointed toward the bridal necklace he wore. "And throw them into harems where they're never heard from again."

The amusement didn't leave his eyes. "Death."

"Huh?"

"My name is Death."

Chills worked up and down Kari's spine. Talk about throwing a bucket of ice water over the libido. "So you don't intend to rape me, just fuck me and kill me." She knew her eyes were bulging because they felt ready to pop out of her head. She reached for the button to the pod, preparing to escape through it. "You people are even more barbaric than legend allows, which is saying a lot!"

What the fuck have I done?! Holy shit! I need to get out of here!

Her heart racing, Kari fumbled for the button to the pod, not wanting to take her eyes off the towering, eight-foot threat looming close to her. She ignored the fact he was staring at her as though she were a simpleton.

"Stay back!" Kari yelled, her hand still blindly searching for the escape button. "Nobody is killing me!" Terrified, she gave the giant her back so she could see the pod's control. "His name is Death," she hysterically mumbled to herself while pushing the button. "All the men in Crystal City and I find the serial killer!"

The transporter's doors whizzed open. She ran inside, only to have a muscular arm unforgivingly snatch her back into the penthouse. The scene was hopelessly reminiscent of Ann Darrow attempting to flee from King Kong.

"'Tis my name, High Lord Death," he grunted. "'Tis not a bedamned metaphor nor a pronouncement of your impending doom."

"Oh my God! Oh my God!" Kari screamed, her body flailing against his hold. Her heart threatened to beat out of her chest. "Somebody help *meeeeee*! A serial kil—" She abruptly stopped kicking and fell limp. She was silent for a long moment while she steadied her breathing. "Your actual name is fucking *Death*?!"

"Nay. Just Death. Not fucking Death."

She frowned at his shitty attempt at humor. "That's the stupidest name I've ever heard! What the hell was your mother thinking, naming you that?! And put me down!"

"'Tis not the name bestowed upon me at birth." He set her on the ground. "'Tis the name I was given by my Master whilst a slave."

Kari blinked. She turned around to face him. His golden gaze had dimmed somewhat, melting the righteous indignation straight out of her. "You were a slave?"

"Aye."

"And now a high lord?"

"Aye."

She shook her head as if to clear it. "Why didn't you discard your slave name and reclaim your birth name?"

"And so I shall when he has died at my hands."

Now he was definitely talking about killing someone, but this time Kari wasn't frightened. Nor could she blame him. The warlord had to be talking about the man who'd once owned him and lord only knows what the giant endured while in chains.

She'd never been more confused in her life. Her brain screamed to run, but her body wanted to stay exactly where it was. The chaotic state of bewilderment she'd been thrust into was dizzying in its force.

Kari had to make a choice and she had to make it now. Listen to her head and obey Klykka as she always did or follow her heart and succumb to eight feet of temptation. Why, why, *why* did this man who haunted her every thought have to be the one species of male she couldn't have?

He must have realized she was in turmoil. The giant slowly ran a massive hand through her hair. "The color of the fire-berry," he softly rumbled. "'Tis as beautiful as you."

Kari closed her eyes and sipped in a few calming breaths. She was tired of fighting him off in her dreams and had even less desire to fend him off in reality. This thrust and parry pretense was exhausting and futile. She knew what she wanted; she'd realized it the first moment she saw him.

Kari opened her eyes and slowly looked up. There would be no more lying to herself or to him, no more running from what "the gift" screamed was right. Klykka might never understand her choice, but neither did The Gy'at Li have to live with the "what-ifs" Kari understood would forever haunt her if she walked away from this moment in time.

She gently cleared her throat. Her gaze searched his. "I'm not calling you 'Death'."

He studied her face. "Why not?"

"Because I've been in this galaxy for seventeen Yessat Years and the only time I've truly felt alive is when you're looking at me."

Silence.

The tension was thick, but the burden of pretending had been lifted from her. When the warrior remained silent, Kari experienced a moment of trepidation from her honesty. In the end, no matter what happened, she decided she wouldn't regret being true to herself.

"Isar," the giant finally murmured. "My name is Isar Kal Draji."

Her eyes softened and her heart skipped a beat. "Isar," Kari whispered. "That's a beautiful name."

"I would that I could put my necklace on you. Leastways, you are safe, *pani*, for I will not test you as a Sacred Mate until the evil has been vanquished."

She had no idea what most of his words meant, but she rightly concluded he wouldn't steal her away and throw her into a harem. She just wished that knowledge felt as liberating as it should.

"You are a virgin," he said thickly.

The sudden change in topic threw her for a moment. "No." She looked away. "It's been a long time, but I'm not a virgin."

"You do not carry the scent of a warrior."

Her head flew back up. "You can smell that?!" Did Trystonni males have heightened senses like animals or something? "And I didn't say I was with a warrior."

"A humanoid of a lower species?"

Kari frowned. "Of *my* species, yes."

There went his eyes, dancing again. The change would have been imperceptible to anyone not closely studying him.

"My people do not consider wenches of any species to be lowly. Leastways, only their males are below our notice."

Kari swallowed with a little less difficulty. His speech reeked of unintentional arrogance, but she could live with that. It didn't matter what value or lack thereof he placed on male humans because the chances of him ever meeting one was in the zilch-to-nada range. She didn't agree human men were lesser beings than warriors, but she wearily admitted *any* male paled in comparison to the tattooed one standing before her. At least where she was concerned.

"'Twill hurt," Death said.

Kari blinked a few times. She wasn't following his train of thought. "What will hurt?"

"The first time I impale you."

She wet her lips. The apprehension and doubt was returning.

"Leastways, I will be gentle with you when I breach your maidenhead, but once your channel accepts my shaft inside and you are a virgin no more, I make no vow that I can continue to be gentle."

He hadn't even touched her and already she was wet. She blew out a breath.

"Make no mistake, *pani*. You are mine and your virginity belongs to me."

He really viewed her as a virgin. She hesitantly wondered just how well endowed the giant was.

"Remove your *zoka*," Death said thickly. "Then lead me to your bedchamber."

This was everything Kari wasn't supposed to let happen — and everything she wanted more than air to breathe. She raised a beleaguered palm to her forehead. "What the hell is happening to me?" she dramatically wailed. "Seventeen Yessat Years I've been in this crazy place and the first man I'm attracted to is causing me to lose what's left of my mind!"

"Remove your *zoka* lest I remove it for you."

Her clit pulsed. She shouldn't break her vow to Klykka, but every word he uttered made her arousal grow stronger. "Isar..."

"Don't force me to test you," the warrior warned. His words were spoken in a deep, gravelly timbre with a hint of reverberation—much like a computer-synthesized voice back home—and they made no sense to her. "Do you pass the test, 'twill make it nigh unto excruciating for the both of us when I must leave to hunt him."

"Test me? I don't understand what you're talking—hey!"

Kari yelped as her *zoka* and sandals fell to the ground. She was completely naked. "What the hell happ— Did you do this?" Nobody had warned her that Trystonni warriors possessed telekinetic powers! She was clearly out of her league here. "How did you..."

The giant's expression, for once not stoic, looked pained. She didn't understand anything that was happening, or why being able to remove her clothing with his mind was significant to him, but for reasons she couldn't explain the thought of him hurting was unbearable. Her face softened. "Isar..."

"You are mine," he rasped out, "yet I cannot claim you. 'Tis cruel irony, this."

Kari had no idea what he was talking about, but the emotional pain he was suffering caused her heart to wrench. His glowing, golden eyes dimmed again—an indication she'd come to realize meant he was in agony. "Isar," she murmured, "I don't understand…"

"'Tis best you don't. I shall carry this burden alone, *pani*."

Kari's gentle gaze soaked up the sight of the man standing before her. Isar was eight feet tall and probably four to five hundred pounds of solid, honed muscle. His dark hair was inky black and, she remembered from the night at Mettle Tavern, silky to the touch. His golden-brown skin, so sexy, accentuated the golden hue of his again glowing eyes. His jaw, rigid and masculine, was perfect in its angularity. Even the skull tattooed onto his forehead, which had undoubtedly been branded on him by the bastard who'd once enslaved him, only added to his appeal. It was barbarically tribal in appearance, the skull figure only apparent by the lines and curves that formed it when standing close to him. The black leather vest he wore called attention to his powerful chest and arms. The matching leather pants failed to hide his intimidating musculature, as well as his massive erection.

Kari bit her lip. She hadn't even seen his penis yet, but judging by the obvious bulge, she doubted he'd fit inside her without killing her.

"Do not fear me, little one," Isar murmured. "I would never bring harm to you."

"I know," she quietly admitted.

Kari hesitated for a brief moment. She had promised The Gy'at Li she would never do this, but when the vow had been made Kari couldn't have possibly realized the powerful effect this man would have on her. She could feel his emptiness, his loneliness, as if it were a tangible thing. That shared experience only made the inexplicable bond between them stronger.

Her decision made, Kari turned around and slowly walked toward her bedchamber. Though his footfalls were silent with the practiced skill of a fierce hunter, she knew without looking back that he was following her. When she entered the bedchamber, Kari wasted no time in getting straight to the point. Climbing onto the large *vesha* bed, she turned to face him and sat back on her heels.

Isar said nothing, but his blazing eyes said everything. His gaze flicked from her face, to her breasts, to her pussy, and back again. He took his time studying every inch of her, her arousal increasing as he did so. She felt like he was attempting to memorize everything about her so in his darkest, emptiest moments he'd be able to recall their time together with complete clarity. She couldn't say she didn't understand why because she was doing the same thing to him.

They were two lost souls who'd finally found their way home. Both of their futures might have lain elsewhere, but for whatever time they had left together, they could both experience, at long last, the completion they felt only in each other's presence.

"I want you, Isar," Kari said softly. "I've never wanted anyone the way I want you."

Their gazes clashed. His eyes, always so haunted, glowed with emotion. "I want you too, Kari," the warlord admitted in a quiet rumble. "No matter what happens, always know 'tis only you I love."

Tears sprang to her eyes. Had those words been uttered by any other man she would have called bullshit, yet she knew that where Isar was concerned there was no pretense. He meant everything he said. The entire situation was emotional and confusing. She didn't understand how she'd turned into a soothsayer where this warrior was concerned, but then neither did she understand Trystonni mating. If *this* is what the stolen Galian women of lore had felt, she doubted they put up much resistance to their alleged kidnappings.

One moment Isar had been fully clothed and a blink of an eye later he was as naked as Kari. The initial shock of once again witnessing his ability to telekinetically do things like that was quickly replaced by the ever-tightening knot of arousal in her belly. Her breath caught in the back of her throat as her silver-blue gaze drank up the sight of him. He was beautiful.

His massive arms were riddled with tribal tattoos, while his sculpted torso and long, muscled legs were devoid of them. When he turned around for a brief moment to kick his clothes away, she noted that his back was the most heavily tattooed part of him.

Kari's pulse raced. Everything about him was perfect.

Isar's cock, so thick and long, was even sexier than she'd imagined it would be while masturbating to thoughts of him thrusting it inside her. Kari blew out a breath as the giant warlord made his way toward her. Shivering with anticipation, her nipples hardened as he got on the bed and joined her on his knees. As they continued memorizing each other's bodies, it occurred to Kari that she'd never felt more desired or cherished.

She came up on her knees and reached for his neck, wanting to put her arms around him. Understanding, Isar craned his neck and lowered himself to the extent he could to accommodate her. "Kari…"

"They took my name from me too," she admitted. "Please, just when we're alone, call me by my birth name. Call me Kara."

His eyes widened almost imperceptibly. With Isar being a native of Tryston, she could tell that further explanation of why her name had been taken from her wasn't necessary.

"Whilst alone then," Isar murmured, "'tis Kara."

She could have cried. Instead she threw her arms around him and reached up to kiss him.

His mouth came down on top of hers, his tongue immediately demanding entry. She took him in, his moan intoxicating, as he wrapped her in his powerful embrace and kissed her with the passion of a thousand men. Her hand, so tiny by comparison, found his cock and began stroking it.

"Kara," he gasped, tearing his mouth from hers, "I needs be inside you now, *pani*."

His breathing was already labored. Perspiration dotted his brow. Seeing her effect on him was as intoxicating as it was heady.

"Then fuck me, Isar," she boldly whispered. "Because I need you too."

He gently prodded her down onto her back, his heavy body coming to rest between her thighs. His calloused fingers played with her pussy hair before trailing up to massage her stiff nipples. She whimpered as he toyed with her, never so turned on in her life.

"I'll come back to these nipples that belong to me later," he half growled. Bending his neck, he sucked on one and then the other as though he couldn't help himself. She groaned and pulled his head in closer. He sucked on her nipple for another few seconds before releasing it with a popping sound.

"Fuck me, Isar," she breathed out. "*Please.*"

Her words, dirty in every language, drove him crazy with desire. His teeth gritting, he held his cock by the shaft and guided it toward her wet entrance. Kari's eyes widened when she felt the head try to get inside her. He was too massive—it wasn't going to fit.

"'Twill be all right, Kara," Isar thickly promised. His heavy-lidded eyes signified a gnawing lust. "'Twill hurt for a short time, but then will be naught but pleasure." He placed a quick kiss on her forehead. "'Tis a vow amongst..." His voice trailed off. She could feel his emotional pain again. "'Tis a vow," he said simply.

Kari no longer cared about the impending physical pain. She just wanted Isar's sadness to disappear. "I trust you," she whispered, smiling up at him. She didn't understand why she did, but her words were honest. "I trust you."

Isar's gaze searched hers. His jaw tightened. "One day you will wear my necklace," he promised her. "I'm sorry, Kara."

"Sorry for wh—"

Kari screamed as Isar impaled her, seating himself to the hilt. She instinctively flailed beneath him, trying in vain to remove him.

"Shhh shhh," he said thickly, "'twill make it worse do you move."

She didn't think there was such a thing as worse, but didn't wish to test the theory either. Against her volition, tears stung her eyes. "It hurts," she gasped, embarrassed by the child-like tremble in her voice. "Really badly."

For whatever reason, he seemed turned on by her tears. She decided it had to be a Trystonni male thing. Going where no other warrior had gone before and all that.

"Tell me when your channel adjusts to my cock," Isar hoarsely instructed her. His jaw was clenched, every muscle in his body flexed with tension. "By the goddess, Kara, your tight pussy feels so good."

His erotic words worked like an aphrodisiac. As the stabbing sensation between her thighs eased and the stinging tears calmed, her body began to relax. "It's better," she told him. "It doesn't hurt as bad."

It was all the coaxing he needed. Isar's nostrils flared as he began to slowly move inside her.

He hadn't lied. The pain was turning into pleasure. She had no idea how such was possible, but neither did she care.

"Oh my God," Kari breathed out. "Yesss."

He picked up the pace, his small movements turning into full, possessive strokes. His cock plunged in and out of her tight pussy, over and over, again and again. Her eyes slowly closed as her head lolled back on the *vesha* hide.

"Look at me, Kara," Isar hoarsely commanded. "I want to know 'tis only I you see."

Kari forced her eyes open. Their gazes, so animalistic now, clashed and held. She moaned as he fucked her, her tits jiggling beneath him with each thrust. Her pulse raced. "Harder," she demanded between gasps, "faster."

His teeth gritting, Isar complied. He fucked her pussy harder, primitive growls erupting from his throat. He impaled her over and over, again and again, fucking her as if he meant to brand her. "Mine," he territorially ground out. *"Only mine."*

Perspiration-slicked skin slapped against perspiration-slicked skin. The sound of her pussy getting thoroughly owned permeated the bedchamber, turning her on impossibly more. Kari entered the void on a loud groan, unable to stop herself from pulling Isar into arousal-lock with her had she wanted to.

Their gazes remained clashed, blazing with primitive intensity. They groaned together as they fucked fast and hard. He was experiencing her arousal which heightened his own, and she was experiencing his, further intensifying hers. She hadn't known the latter was possible, but was too turned on to consider what that could mean.

"I'm coming," Kari gasped, gluttonously indulging in his every stroke. He fucked her harder. *"Isar, I'm—oh god!"*

The knot of arousal in her belly snapped, forcing Kari to orgasm on a loud moan. Blood rushed to her nipples, causing them to stab out. Blood rushed to her clit, escalating its sensitivity.

Isar growled as he plunged in and out of her tight, wet cunt. She threw her hips back at him, fucking him as hard as he was fucking her. She experienced his arousal as though it was her own, forcing a second, harder orgasm out of her.

"This pussy is mine," he ground out, his jawline flexed. *"Mine."*

He sank into her flesh harder, impaling her cunt with deep, fast strokes. She felt his entire body tense over hers, his teeth gritting, as he plunged inside her. He fucked her like he owned her, thrusting in and out once, twice, three times more. *"Kara."*

Isar came on a possessive roar, his massive body juddering over hers. Kari screamed from the intensity of the arousal-lock, coming a third, brutal time as his hot cum exploded inside her, filling her with his seed. Even then he didn't stop fucking her, his cock still hard as steel. He impaled her over and over and over, the pleasure driving her near to delirium. He fucked her harder, deeper, and faster until, on a growl of completion, he came again.

Kari's final climax, a culmination of all their orgasms, was so intense as to be painful. Still in arousal-lock, Isar experienced everything she did. They yelled out their pleasure-pain as they came simultaneously, the ferociousness of their shared orgasm powerful enough to split an atom.

Panting from exhaustion, Kari broke the arousal-lock. She smiled as the warlord fell onto his back beside her and pulled her up to sleep on his chest. They said nothing as they held onto each other.

One enormous hand rubbed her ass cheeks as the other one played with her hair. They fell into a deep slumber, both of them complete for the first time in their lives.

Chapter Eleven

Kari awoke the next morning only to find that Isar Kal Draji was no longer in her bed. She sat up and bit her lip. Knowing his departure was for the best didn't dull the stinging aftereffects of said disappearance. If she were honest with herself, it hurt knowing that the warlord had no problem leaving her without so much as a goodbye after the night they'd spent together.

Isar had fucked Kari like a branded animal, taking her more times and in more ways than she'd once believed possible. In her mouth, up her ass, in her pussy, between her tits...

And that was only recounting the first two hours.

His hard thrusts had been possessive, his thickly murmured words statements of ownership. She'd never felt so wanted, so needed, in her entire life.

When he'd finally felt replete and completely satiated, the warlord had latched his mouth onto one of her nipples and suckled it as he slept. She'd run her fingers through his silky, black hair until she too had passed out. She had expected to wake up to him kissing, licking, and sucking all over her body, but instead she had awoken to loneliness.

Sighing, Kari pulled herself out of bed. Her entire body ached. Slowly lumbering toward the bathing chamber, she looked around the penthouse en route, hoping the giant hadn't left her after all and was merely sitting on the veranda with his breakfast. The thought cheered her so she forced her sore muscles to move a bit faster. Half expecting to see Isar and half expecting to not, her stomach lurched when she discovered it was the latter. She closed her eyes for a moment and took a calming breath.

This is for the best, Kari, and you damn well know it. He knows it too.

Her eyes flicked open. With a heavy heart, Kari Gy'at Li walked into the bathing chamber.

* * * * *

The chamber must have sensed her aching body needed a hot bath because that's exactly what it gave her. The heated water was infused with healing sands imported from Tryston, rejuvenating her body even if her mind hadn't quite reached that point yet.

What did you expect, Kari? Klykka warned you not to become involved with a Trystonni warrior...

But that warning had been necessary because of their penchant for stealing women, not abandoning them. Of all the warriors in Tryston, Kari thought with downturned lips, she fell for the one who wasn't into abduction. Not that she wanted kidnapped, but it would have done a lot for her ego if he'd at least damn tried.

She rubbed her temples. "He's driven me insane," she muttered. "I don't want thrown into some fucking harem."

A few minutes later, Kari alighted from the bathing chamber scrubbed clean, pussy hair trimmed, body pain-free and dry, and red-wine ringlets perfectly coiffed. She really had to talk Klykka into installing one of those babies back home. It was the one technological gadget in Crystal City she'd miss.

"Incoming holo-call from Arista de Valor. Shall I connect her holograph, Kari Gy'at Li?"

Kari took a deep breath before answering the unseen computer-like mechanism that controlled everything in the penthouse. She had wanted to name it "Mother" just like the spaceship's computer in *Alien*, but the damn thing had a mind of its own. "Yes, of course. Connect her, Rumschlag."

Rumschlag. What the fuck kind of a name was that? It reminded her of some drunken German doing the chicken dance at Oktoberfest.

Arista's holo-image zapped into existence. The High Mystik absently glanced over Kari's naked body. "You've just availed yourself of the bathing chamber. 'Tis bliss, is it not?"

"I was just trying to figure out how to talk Klykka into installing one back in our sector." Kari grinned. "So the answer is a raging *yes*."

Arista smiled. "Leastways, are you enjoying your holiday in Crystal City?"

"Yeah. Sure."

One royal eyebrow arched. "Your tone does not match your words. You have the sound of Rumschlag."

"What is wrong with my voice?"

"It's monotone," Kari said grumpily. She waved a hand toward the unseen computer. "Privacy, please."

"Fine. Leastways, my voice is all things sexy and wondrous."

Kari rolled her eyes.

"I would that you could confide in me, child."

Arista's expression was soft and her tone concerned. For some reason that made Kari feel like weeping and confessing all, but the High Mystik would undoubtedly think she'd lost her mind for ever getting into this position in the first place.

"'Tis the giant warrior, aye?"

Kari's head shot up. Her eyes rounded.

"A simpleton I am not," Arista mused. "Leastways, I saw the way you looked at him."

"You should have seen the way she mated with him. 'Twas nigh unto obscene."

"Enough, Rumschlag," Kari gritted out. She cleared her throat and gave The de Valor her full attention. "Well it's nothing to worry about. He's gone anyway."

"Worried? Nay. I was never worried. You are too skilled to be taken against your will."

"I never got the chance to test that theory," she sniffed. "Apparently I'm not worthy of a Trystonni kidnapping!"

"Mayhap he knew you are too strong."

"Mayhap he thought you too perverse."

"Well he could have tried! And for the final time, Rumschlag, shut the fuck up!"

"As you desire. Leastways, I have duties to attend to."

"So attend to them already!"

"You desire to become the warlord's chattel?" Arista asked, ignoring Kari's little spat with the computer.

Yes. "No!" Kari sighed. Maybe Isar truly had driven her to the brink of insanity. If so, Rumschlag had pushed her over the precipice. "I don't share. If I ever—what do you call it here?—*mate*...I'll be the only woman my husband has sex with, period."

"As well it should be."

"Anyway," Kari said, changing the still too fresh subject, "I'll be fine." She forced a smile. "Why did you call?"

"Ahh that." Arista inclined her head. "'Tis expected that Mettle Tavern will be overflowing with patrons this eve. Leastways, the warriors who come every few moon-months to barter their healing sands have arrived."

"You need me to serve trenchers? Sure." *It's not like I have anything else to do!* "I'll be there at suns-down."

"I need you to perform. For a certainty you are the most skilled at it and 'tis a boon do we keep these warriors calmed and tame."

Kari nodded. "You got it. I'll see you tonight."

Arista prepared to end the holo-communication when a thought struck Kari. It was a scenario she had mulled over again and again, but kept forgetting to inquire about it. "Completely unrelated to anything we've just discussed, I was wondering if I could ask you a question?"

"For a certainty."

"I hope this doesn't make me sound weak or like the child you and Klykka call me…"

"Just ask."

"What if I don't want to be a High Mystik?"

Arista's eyes widened.

"I don't mean that in a bad way!" Kari quickly corrected. "I want to be a High Mystik someday, just not so soon."

Arista's lips formed an O. "You've but one final step to complete your training, yet you are unready to leave Klykka and rule o'er a sector of your own. Correct?"

"I know it sounds weak," Kari sheepishly admitted, "but yeah. I'm not ready to leave the woman who took me in and made me a part of her family."

"'Tis not weak, child. Leastways, you *are* still a child and there is naught wrong with that. For a certainty you are not the first to find herself in this predicament and you shan't be the last."

"It's possible to finish my training and not be a High Mystik then?"

"More or less, aye." Arista thought that over. "You shall retain the title of Mystik until you are ready to rule your own sector. Even though you'll have the skills of a High Mystik in deed, only she who rules in name as well as deed is awarded the power and voting rights that come with it."

Kari blew out a breath of relief. "I just hope Klykka accepts my decision."

"She will. Leastways, 'twill like as not serve to further endear you to her."

Kari hoped so, but didn't say as much. She knew The de Valor's time was precious and didn't want to waste any more of it with her selfish concerns. "Thank you, Arista. I'll see you tonight."

The holo-call came to an end. Lost in thought, Kari absently stared at where The de Valor's image had been but moments prior.

"Do not perform for those warriors," a deep voice said harshly. "'Tis a command, that."

Kari whirled around. Her eyes widened and her heart raced. She tried not to smile, but she knew it didn't matter—the weird bond they shared told him she was happy to see him.

"I thought you were gone," Kari said, her head notching up. He hadn't left her without saying goodbye after all! "I woke up to an empty bed."

"I was. I went to the bartering stalls to buy food." Isar's golden gaze possessively raked over her naked body. "Leastways, I would have starved had I known whilst in my absence you would agree to perform this moon-rising."

"Food?" She shook her head. "I could have ordered you any food you wanted and it would have been instantly prepared."

"I did not know this."

"Well thank you for buying food. That was thoughtful of you."

He grunted in response. She smiled.

"How did you get back in here?" Kari asked. "You don't have the proper laser scan."

"I've my ways." He shifted the bags of food in his arms to draw attention to them. "Let us eat so I've the energy to fuck what's mine again."

Kari blew out a breath. The warlord's blunt words aroused her more than they probably should have. She inclined her head and led the way to the terrace where she took her meals. She could sense him following behind her, his eyes all but burning a brand into her buttocks.

"I have to perform," Kari said as she led him into the terrace's gardens. "I gave Arista my word." When they reached her favorite table, she turned to face him. "And I don't break my word."

Isar frowned. "Then I will accompany you this eve," he grumbled. "Leastways, you will touch no warrior but me."

She didn't want to anyway, but pretended to strike a bargain. "Fair enough." She sat down at the table and watched him pull an array of delicious foods from the crystal-spun bags. Her mouth started to water. "But we can't have penetration there. Only oral sex."

"Nay. I want all there to know you belong to me."

"They cannot know," Kari told him. She picked up a sticky breakfast treat that reminded her of the pastries back home. "I'd get in trouble with my Mistress. Galians disallow their females to have intercourse with Trystonni warriors."

One black eyebrow shot up. "Why?"

"Because your kind has stolen Galian females in the past." She bit into the *felani*. "This is really good."

His eyes were amused. "Do I penetrate you at Mettle Tavern they will think I would kidnap you?"

"Yes."

"Mayhap I will."

Kari almost choked on her second bite of *felani*. She fiddled with some buttons on the table and *pici* juice instantly appeared. She quickly drank some down. His gaze, still amused, watched her every movement. Once recovered, she gave him a stern frown.

"Me almost dying is funny to you?"

"I would never let you die, *pani*. Leastways, do you die, I die."

Kari begrudgingly experienced a thrill from his admission. Metaphorical or not, it made her pulse race pleasurably. She studied his handsome face and didn't know how she'd ever say goodbye to him.

"When I take my leave from Galis, 'tis mine you still are. Touch no other male."

She grunted. "I'm supposed to be a nun when you leave?"

"What is a nun?"

"Never mind." She took another big bite of *felani*. "Will you be with other females?"

"Only if needs be. Leastways, I will keep to the *Kefa* slaves."

"One, it's wrong to own slaves. And two, if you're fucking other females I'm fucking whoever I want!"

"You are fucking no male and the slaves are not real!" he barked. "How can you know naught of the *Kefas*?"

Kari was getting a headache. "You fuck invisible female slaves?"

Isar frowned at her sarcasm. "They are made of the colored *trelli* sands and enchanted by priestesses for unmated warriors to mount."

"Tryston sounds too weird," she muttered. "Look. I love spending this time with you, but we both know it will come to an end."

"For mayhap a spell," he conceded. "I would that I could take you as my Sacred Mate now." He sighed. "Leastways, for your own safety, I cannot."

Kari didn't know what he was talking about, but she was too sad to give it more thought. Whether Isar understood or not, she could never truly belong to him. Such would be a slap in the face to the High Mystik who'd adopted her as her own. She wished there was a way to have it all, but knew it wasn't possible. Even if Kari chose to defy Klykka, which she couldn't fathom doing, she realized she could never be happy living out her life on a planet where women were mere possessions. And a warrior such as Isar? He would never be able to accept the lowly status of men on Galis. Both planets were fucked up in their own ways.

They had a week left together, maybe ten days at best. Kari wanted to savor every moment of it with him because she realized she would never feel for any man what she felt when Isar Kal Draji looked at her.

"Do not be sad, *pani*," Isar murmured, "for it makes me sad when you are."

"I'm trying not to be," Kari whispered, "but we both know our time together is nearing its end."

"Only for a while."

Kari knew differently, but said nothing. She morosely decided the plot of *Romeo and Juliet* was too close to home for her liking.

Standing up, she walked to where the warlord sat. She got on her knees and fumbled with his leather pants until his long, thick, hard cock sprang free. She looked up and met his glowing gaze while she stroked his shaft. His intake of breath was quickly followed by a massive hand entwining its fingers in her hair.

"Fuck me with your mouth," Isar said hoarsely. "I needs be close to you."

"Don't ever forget me," Kari murmured, her heart wrenching, "because I'll never forget you."

He opened his mouth to speak. "Shhh," Kari said softly, "right now we have each other and it's all I need."

She lowered her head and took his cock into her mouth. His low growl of approval made her want to please him all the more. She slowly began sucking his shaft, taking in as much of him as was humanly possible.

"Kara," he hissed. His fingers wrapped tighter around her tendrils of hair. "Suck him hard, *pani*."

Her nipples stiffened at his provocative words. She picked up the pace, sucking his cock in fast, deep strokes. His groans of pleasure mingled with the sound of wet mouth meeting rigid flesh. Her head bobbed up and down as she ferociously sucked him off, ready and wanting to taste his cum.

"*Faster*," Isar gritted out. "I'm almost there, *pani*."

Kari sucked his cock harder and faster, her throat opening for his huge erection. She took him in impossibly deeper while maintaining a feverish pace. She fucked him with her wet mouth, over and over, again and again. When his entire body tensed, she sucked even harder, her head wildly bobbing up and down.

"I'm coming," he said thickly. "*I'm com—*"

Isar came on a roar, his flexed body convulsing, as he spurted his hot cum into her mouth. Kari moaned as she drank him, her mouth and throat still sucking him off, milking him of everything he had to give. She kept sucking and sucking, like a grown baby on a bottle, until a harder, final spurt of cum erupted in her mouth. He groaned as she eagerly drank from him, loving the taste of his seed.

His breathing was ragged, his skin slick with perspiration. The moment her mouth stopped milking him, he lifted her onto his lap. Kari plunged down onto his cock, her tight pussy enveloping him, causing both of them to moan. The warrior lowered his head and sucked on her erect nipples like lollipops while she rode him to orgasm.

"And so you know?" Isar said, panting. "For a certainty I love your perversions."

Kari grinned and kept riding him.

Chapter Twelve

"I asked you *not* to penetrate me," Kari hissed as the pod spat them back out into Klykka's Crystal City palace. "But you did. What if Arista tells my sister?!"

"I seem to recall you begged me for it," Isar reminded her. His stance and timbre reeked of arrogance. "Leastways, the hard fucking I gave you knocked out every bedamned warrior within an hour of Crystal City."

Kari agitatedly ran a hand through her long mane of curls. "Only because you got me so worked up. You could have saved that for when we got back here, you know."

"Aye."

She frowned at his admission. He had told her he wanted everyone to know she belonged to him and had taken it upon himself to demonstrate as much. Now when called out on it, he unapologetically confirmed he had done so. She sighed. She supposed the bright side was the warrior didn't bother with lying.

"Kara," Isar said thickly, calling her by her birth name. He took her hand and placed it on the bulge in his leather pants. She could feel his massive erection beneath her palm. "I needs be inside you."

Kari wet her lips. It wasn't natural to be this horny thirty *Nuba*-minutes after engaging in sex. She didn't understand the effect this man had on her, but she was tired of trying to analyze it. "You're driving me insane."

"Insane?"

"Mad, daft."

"I'm already there," Isar murmured. "'Tis a boon do we go daft together."

Kari half snorted and half laughed. "That doesn't even make sense." She grinned, her dimples showing, as she squeezed his erection. "But you're so sexy I'll let you get away with it."

His expression grew serious. "I love you, Kara. No matter what fate decides, know that I always will."

Her hand dropped to her side. Her gaze softened. She could feel his pain again as though it were her own. "I love you too, Isar, and I always will."

The warlord picked her up as though she weighed no more than a flower and carried her into the bedchamber. Their sex that night wasn't rough and animalistic, but all-consuming and emotional.

Isar had given her another first. Until this night, Kari had no idea what it felt like to make love.

* * * * *

Kari had stopped keeping track of the days and no longer knew how many had passed. Seven? Nine? Ten thousand? It didn't matter; she could never get enough of Isar Kal Draji. And therein lay the problem.

The more time she spent in his presence, the more difficult the idea of separating from him became. Their holiday together was a hairsbreadth from ending. Once upon a time she'd been heartbroken when she thought he'd left Galis without saying goodbye; now Kari wondered if that parting farewell was a word she could handle hearing.

"Maybe I should leave Crystal City now, while Isar is out attending to business," she murmured to herself. Her heart was heavy — and broken. "At least then I could pretend it's not *goodbye* and only a *to be continued*." Sighing, she sank down into her favorite *vesha*-soft crystal chair on the balcony. "I don't know what I'm doing anymore."

"Mayhap you are desirous of my counsel?"

"Not really," Kari said, her voice as monotone as Rumschlag's, "but I'm sure you'll give it to me anyway."

"Like as not, aye."

Kari grunted. "You barely spoke when I arrived in Crystal City. Hell, you didn't even tell me how the bathing chamber worked or how to order food for that matter! Now you rarely shut up. I'm starting to wax nostalgic for the old days."

"'Tis rubber I am, 'tis glue you are."

Kari plopped her elbow onto the table and her chin onto her palm. "Your English is improving at least. Go on. Counsel away."

"'Twill injure the warlord's feelings do you take your leave without giving him your farewell, yet 'twill pain you sorely do you say it to him."

"Thanks for the recap. You're a regular Oracle of Delphi."

"I know naught of this Oracle, yet I recognize sarcasm when I hear it. Do you desire my counsel or nay?"

Kari sighed. She really had nothing to lose. "Okay, Rumschlag. I'm listening."

"I have run all the variables and calculated all the probabilities in 30,000,000,105 known mathematical systems. Leastways, you should take your leave of Crystal City the soonest."

"I don't want to hurt him," she whispered.

"Leave a holo-message with me and I shall give it to the High Lord upon his return."

Kari closed her eyes.

"I sense you wish to gaze upon him a final time, yet my calculations assure me 'tis wiser do you not."

"Because I'll hurt even more than I otherwise would?" Assuming that was in the realm of possibility. "Or because it'll hurt us both?"

"Probability suggests that when faced with the reality of separation, the warlord will defy the path the goddess has decreed and steal you away from Galis."

Kari's pulse picked up. She lifted her head. "Really?"

"'Tis foolhardy do you give him this opportunity, even do you desire it. Leastways, he can never truly be free of the mental chains that bind him do you not force his hand that he might walk the path the goddess has so decreed."

The former master Isar had spoken of. The one he was determined to track down and eradicate.

"You will be all hindrance and no help, Kari Gy'at Li, for you've still to complete your training in the warring arts."

"Can you read my damn mind?" Kari asked, her irritation apparent. She rubbed her weary temples. "Don't answer that. I'm sure I don't want to know."

"I sense that you are desirous of matpow. Shall I have a carafe delivered?"

"Make it two, Rumschlag," Kari muttered. She sighed. "I have a feeling I'm going to need it."

* * * * *

Safely ensconced in her rooms back in the Gy'at Li sector, Kari didn't know whether or not she wished to see the holo-image Rumschlag had transmitted to her. She'd been back home for nearly a week and had been in possession of the as yet unviewed transmission for almost as long. It was time to make a choice. Klykka and Dorra were expected to return from their pack-hunt in a mere few *Nuba*-hours. If she wanted to view the holo-image without worrying someone would walk in on her while watching it, the time to do so was now.

Kari nibbled at her bottom lip, an anxious quirk she'd developed this past week. One of the manservants had even commented on it, pointing out how raw her mouth looked. She couldn't help it. Every time she contemplated Isar's possible reactions, she unconsciously resumed the biting. Was Isar angry? Hurt? Unaffected? Unfortunately, none of the possibilities would make her feel better. And yet…

"Who am I kidding?" Kari whispered to the walls. "I have to know what happened. I'll drive myself crazy otherwise."

She took a deep, steadying breath. As prepared as she ever would be, Kari reached out a shaky hand and pressed the button. The recorded memory instantly zinged to life.

"I'm sorry I ran, Isar."

Kari watched her hologram spill out her apology to the warlord. Her heart raced just seeing him again, even if it was only in holo-memory.

"I just couldn't bear to hear you say goodbye. Nor could I bear saying that word to you. Just know that I will never forget you and I will keep the memories of our time together close to my heart."

Isar reached out a heavily muscled arm, his hand extending as if wanting to touch her, though he realized she wasn't actually there. Kari's eyes filled with unshed tears. She knew too well how he felt.

"You have a path you must walk and a destiny to fulfill. I fear that my presence will only serve to distract you from that goal. You deserve to be whole again. You deserve to feel worthy of your birth name."

He said nothing, only listened, but his eyes blazed with emotion.

"When you love someone—I mean truly love that person with all that you are—their happiness becomes more important to you than your own. This is the love I have for you, Isar Kal Draji. And this is why I had to leave."

The warlord lifted his hand to her holographic face. He wanted to wipe away the single tear that had spilled down her cheek. Kari watched in silence, the scene as humbling as it was heart-wrenching.

"Whether our paths are destined to cross again in this lifetime or whether we must wait to be reunited at the Rah, know that I will always—always—love you." Her final words were a whisper. "Goodbye, my love."

Kari couldn't stop the tears from flowing as Isar spoke to her hologram.

"I love you too, pani." His voice caught in his throat. "Goodbye, my beloved."

The recorded memory zapped out of existence. Kari collapsed onto her bed and sat there unblinking. She stared at nothing for a long moment, praying the numbness she felt would stay.

It didn't. Kari Gy'at Li, born Kara Summers, slid to the floor of her bedchamber. The tears turned to weeping and the weeping into body-racking sobs of anguish. She was completely and irrevocably broken.

Chapter Thirteen

Two Moon-risings Outside Khan-Gori Airspace

Zyrus Galaxy, Seventh Dimension

6049 Y.Y. (Yessat Years)

Kari Gy'at Li studied Princess Dari Q'ana Tal's wide-eyed expression. She'd finished telling her story and the princess looked ready to faint. Out of all the horrors Dari had endured, surely Kari's life story wasn't *that* freaky. She hesitated. Her deductive reasoning skills were usually spot-on, but this situation eluded her.

"Dari," Kari said, "Why are you so upset? Is it—oh damn." She sucked in a gulp of air through her teeth. "I've already considered the possibility that the evil Isar was hunting is the same one we hunt now. My training in the warring arts was completed long ago so I'm more formidable an adversary than I once was."

"I feared as much. About the evil one I mean. Leastways, 'tis not the cause of my upset."

Kari's face scrunched up. "Then what is?" Her eyes rounded as the answer struck her. "I forgot you are still a virgin. I shouldn't have been so graphic in the details." She grimaced. "Forgive me?"

The princess's mouth worked up and down, but no words came out. Kari stared at her quizzically, not understanding Dari's reaction.

Kara—the very high princess whose birth had required Kari to change her name—had been taken in by the Gy'at Lis as one of their own. Before Kara's Sacred Mate had tracked her down in Galis, she'd lived many years in Klykka's stronghold. Kara's stories of Tryston had been terrifying, but enlightening. As such, Kari knew that Trystonni females were accustomed to seeing decadent displays of sexuality so hearing about them shouldn't be this anxiety-provoking.

"'Tis true I am a virgin," Dari stuttered out, "yet I find naught offensive in your tale."

Kari frowned. One wine-red eyebrow inched up. "Then what is wrong, sweetheart? I'm confused."

Dari's glowing blue eyes were round as saucers. Her hands were shaking. By the time the young princess made eye contact with her, Kari felt as nervous as Dari looked. She swallowed heavily.

"What is it?" Kari whispered. "Tell me."

"There is something you needs must know. Leastways, there are several things." The princess took a deep breath. "For a certainty I know not where to begin."

Kari's eyes were as wide as Dari's. A chill worked up and down her spine. "Begin anywhere, but please do start."

Dari inclined her head. She was quiet for a long moment before she finally spoke. "The sister you mourn, the one you say has been dead for mayhap hundreds of Earth years?"

"Kyra." Kari's gaze fell to her lap. Hundreds of thousands of Earth years could go by and the pain would still be as fresh as it was the day she arrived on Galis. She sighed before raising her head to meet Dari's gaze. "My sister's name is Kyra."

"Your name was taken from you."

Kari's forehead crinkled. "What does that have to do with—"

"Please," Dari said, holding up a palm, "let me say all what needs be said."

"Okay," she replied, her voice lowering in timbre. "I'm listening."

"Your name was taken from you upon the birth of the High Princess Kara Q'ana Tal. 'Tis an odd name in Trek Mi Q'an, Kara is." At Kari's nod, Dari continued. "Kara, my cousin, was named by her *mani*—mother."

"I realize we're conversing in Galian, but I speak Trystonni fluently. I know that *mani* means mother."

"Kara's *mani*, the empress, named her in deference to the memory of her dead, beloved sister."

Kari rubbed her temples. "Dari, that's a sweet story, but we have a lot of important matters to discuss. Every moment brings us closer to Khan-Gor if indeed this planet even exists! I need to know what awaits us there." Her expression softened. "You're a sweet girl telling me heartwarming stories, but right now I'm more concerned with keeping you and Bazi alive than with—"

"The empress' name is Kyra," Dari interrupted. "Kyra Q'ana Tal." She grasped Kari's hand. "She was born in first dimension Earth by the birth name of Summers."

Kari's eyes widened. Her heart raced and her breathing grew labored. "Why would you say this?" she gasped, pulling her hand from Dari's grasp. "Is this some cruel joke? What the—"

"My *mani* was also born in the first dimension," Dari continued, undeterred. "Her name then was Geris Jackson, daughter of Hera Jackson. Hera was a famed singer on a planet called Broadway."

"I never told you about Hera," Kari breathed out, her voice guttural. She sounded like a wounded animal. "You

157

couldn't have known that." Her eyes were wild, her face drained of color. "Unless…"

Dari removed the anklet she wore, a bangle with a single holo-charm dangling from it. She handed it to Kari. "Look through the holo-images in the charm," the princess softly instructed. Her glowing blue eyes were filled with emotion. *"Please."*

Kari's hands shook as she accepted the charm. Everything felt surreal, like it was happening to someone else.

She turned the charm on and the holo-images zapped to life. Her heart raced faster as a three-dimensional photograph of two best friends opened before her. "Oh my God," Kari murmured, her voice hoarse. The strongest chill she'd ever experienced coursed down the length of her spine. "Oh my God."

* * * * *

Meanwhile, also in Zyrus Galaxy…

"Dari's holo-charm has been turned on!" King Kil Q'an Tal announced on a roar. He could hear the heavy footfalls of warriors rushing toward the front of the gastrolight cruiser.

"Leastways, I'm trying to bring up the signal without alerting her."

"Is my hatchling alive?" Kil's brother bellowed. King Dak Q'an Tal ran toward his elder sibling. The anguish he felt from failing to protect his beloved daughter was extreme. "Is my Dari alive?" he growled.

Gio, Dari's betrothed, ran beside Dak. The desperation he felt just to see her holo-image was apparent to any warrior who looked upon him. "If she has passed through the Rah," he rasped, "'tis my desire to reunite with her there."

"Cease this bedamned talk of doom!" the emperor shouted. Zor Q'an Tal, the eldest of the brothers, slashed a hand through the air. "'Tis a command!" His teeth gritted as he addressed his brothers and his niece's betrothed. "Leastways, the only warrior on this gastrolight cruiser not driving me nigh into panic is High Lord Death." He absently waved a hand toward the giant in question. "'Twould be wise did the lot of you follow his lead."

Death's golden gaze revealed nothing, but in truth he was mayhap in more agony than all of them combined. All those Yessat Years past, had he held his tongue when the young princess had innocently flirted with him rather than follow the obligatory protocol of debriefing her sire, Dari never would have been removed to Arak and 'twould be safely in Tryston. And then to find out the evil he hunted had been on Arak terrifying Dari all the while...'twas difficult to forgive himself.

Death maintained his composure on the outside, yet felt anything but on the inside. 'Twas the young princess all the warriors fretted over, but he knew for a certainty his unclaimed Sacred Mate would die did it mean saving her. It angered him that the others cared naught of the fate of Kari Gy'at Li, yet neither did they know she belonged to him. Leastways, they should still care. "Does her companion live?" he asked Kil, his voice betraying no emotion.

"Even if she does," Kil answered, "she will still be sent to the gulch pits for aiding and abetting Dari's escape."

Death's jaw tightened. "You would rather Dari be alone than accompanied by a woman skilled in the warring arts?"

"Nay," Kil answered, "but 'tis the holy law."

"Laws can be changed." His glowing golden gaze narrowed at the emperor. "Leastways, do you desire me to continue to rule o'er your sectors, the law *will* be changed."

All the warriors fell silent as they gaped at him. For a certainty High Lord Death was known for his loyalty. That he would throw down a gauntlet against the ruling family of Trek Mi Q'an for a wench was startling.

"Have you gone daft?" Kil asked, bemused. "What does this wench—" His glowing blue gaze widened in comprehension. His jaw dropped. "She belongs to you?"

"She's your Sacred Mate?" the emperor asked, shocked. "The Galian?"

All eyes were trained on High Lord Death, including those of the fourth and final Q'an Tal brother, King Rem, who'd just joined them. None of the warriors had seen this development coming.

"Aye," Death confirmed, "she is."

Silence.

"Why then did you not claim her?" Dak, Dari's sire, asked. "How could you withstand the anguish?"

Anguish was too gentle a word for the bleak emptiness that had consumed him o'er the years. Once a warrior found the only female in all the galaxies who could biologically complete him, being removed from her was the most painful of torture.

"She ran from me," Death admitted.

"A hunter of your skill could have located her." Kil stated what every warrior was thinking. "And you've a lock on her scent does she belong to you."

"Why?" the emperor quietly asked. Zor shook his head as if to clear it. "Leastways, I would that I could understand."

Death hadn't wanted to burden them with what he knew until they caught up with the gastrolight cruiser they were trailing. 'Twould bring naught but more worry to every warrior aboard ship. In the end, he realized he had to tell them for he'd already said too much.

"The one that Dari trails..."

"Who?" Gio growled. "The male in her company?"

"How could Dari follow a male in her company, dunce?" Kil rolled his eyes. "Leastways, I know in my hearts Dari would never betray you. Whoever that male aboard the cruiser is none can say, but she protects him like a mother, not a lover."

Gio's nostrils flared, but he said nothing.

"Dari spoke of an evil," Death continued. "Leastways, I believe she shields the male from it."

Gio's eyebrows drew together. "You believe this evil to be real? 'Tis naught but the imaginings of my runaway bride."

"Nay," Death said softly, "'tis far from imaginary. For a certainty I have been tracking the evil one for more Yessat Years than I care to dwell upon."

"'Tis why you didn't claim your Sacred Mate," the emperor announced, his voice monotone. It was all starting to make sense. "You desired to vanquish this evil afore putting your necklace upon her."

"Aye," Death confirmed. "'Tis true, your words."

The warriors fell silent again as they contemplated the implications. If High Lord Death said the evil one was real then so it was.

"You thought to protect her from the very thing she now chases," Gio said. He stared unblinking, lost in thought. His jaw clenched. "As my betrothed pursues it to protect that bedamned male."

"Mayhap to protect you," Death said pointedly.

Gio blinked. His gaze flew to the High Lord. "Me? She thinks me so weak that—"

"Enough!" Death bellowed, commanding everyone's undivided attention. "For a certainty am I angered listening to your bedamned self-pity." His nostrils flared. "The girl-child obviously loves you for she has sacrificed herself that you might live!"

Gio's eyes rounded.

"You know naught of the evil one," Death ground out. He slashed his hand through the air. "You know naught of its trickery, of its deceptions, or its power! Yet all that consumes you is thoughts of this male in Dari's company—a male who could himself be a child for as much as we know! 'Tis a vow amongst warriors I will kill you myself do you not cease your self-pitying ways and think only of the princess who has shown herself ready to die for you!"

The warriors once again fell into silence. Rem, who'd said nothing up to this point, grunted his approval of Death's verdict.

Gio ran a shaking hand across his jaw. He understood now what Dari had done for him. He fell to his knees in anguish. "I do not deserve her," he rasped out.

Silence.

"Aye you do," Death said quietly. "Leastways, you are a good man and a warrior second to none. But 'tis time to put aside the jealousy of a male removed from his mate and prepare to fight for her."

Gio inclined his head. "Aye. I would die for her."

"We know," Dak said in low tones. His expression betrayed him for who he was—a warrior racked with grief and desperation to find and save his daughter. "Have you been able to harness the holo-charm's signal?" he asked Kil, changing the subject. Dak cleared his throat, obviously trying to steady himself. "Have you seen Dari?"

"I've almost got it," Kil answered. "Just a few more *Nuba-minutes.*"

"How do you know this evil one?" the emperor asked Death. "When did your paths cross?"

All eyes looked to Death. His stoic face didn't betray a hint of the pain wreaking havoc on his insides.

"Our paths crossed," Death murmured, "the day it bought me and named me."

Epilogue

The warriors watched the holographic image Dari's charm provided them with. Gio and Dak breathed in relief when they saw the princess smiling with her female companion as they looked through holo-images together.

Death inhaled deeply, the sight of his beautiful Kari— Kara to him—hitting him with the impact of a *trelli* sandstorm. He had thought he'd made the honorable choice by not claiming his Sacred Mate, yet she was facing more danger now than she would have at his side.

"I'm coming for you, *pani*," Death murmured to himself so none could hear. "This time I will never let you go."

"The audio is coming up!" Kil announced. "Here we go."

All eyes were locked on the holo-display as a boy-child walked over to where the females sat. "Bazi," Dari warmly greeted, "you have awoken."

"Aye." He rubbed his eyes. "Leastways, I had a bad dream."

Gio grimaced, upset with himself for having doubted Dari for even a moment. The male she protected *was* a child.

"Look at the holo-images with us," Kari said. She smiled at Bazi, her dimples popping out. "We're going to turn them off soon."

"Get a lock on their position!" Zor shouted to Kil. The emperor agitatedly ran a hand through his hair. "For a certainty we need that lock afore the signal ends!"

"Hurry," Dak growled, wanting to get to his daughter. "'Tis mayhap but moments left!"

"I'm working on it!" Kil said. "I've got it!"

The holographic display flashed back to Kari. Tears filled her eyes as she looked at Dari's images. None of the warriors knew what to make of that, Death included.

"Look," Kari said softly to Bazi. She held up a holo-image of Zor's wife, Empress Kyra Q'ana Tal. Every warrior's brow furrowed as she reverently ran a finger over the image. "Do you see her, Bazi?"

"Aye. She has the look of you. Leastways, you both have the hair of the fire-berry."

Kari's smile was radiant. A single tear tracked down her cheek. "Do you know why we look so much alike?" she asked.

"Nay," Bazi replied. "Why?"

"Because she's my sister," Kari whispered. Her breath caught in the back of her throat. "The sister I never thought I'd see again when forces I can't understand whisked me from Earth to Galis."

Death stilled. He could hear the emperor's intake of breath without looking to visually confirm it.

"Then we must kill it when we reach Khan-Gor," Bazi said, his chest puffing out. "I will slay the evil for you so you can see your sister again. 'Tis a vow."

Kari ran a protective hand through his hair. "It's time to talk about that."

"Aye," Dari interjected. She sighed. "I shall shut this off so I can tell you the whole of it. We needs must prepare."

The signal came to an abrupt end. The warriors stood there, their expressions as frozen as their bodies. Finally, Kil broke the tense silence with a hearty laugh.

"My brother, the emperor," Kil chortled, "came nigh close to sending his own wife's sister to the gulch pits." At Zor's frown, Kil laughed harder. "'Twould be a lifetime without channel for you, dunce."

Death found his first smile. The rest of the warriors followed suit.

"Put the gastrolight cruiser into hyper-speed," Zor growled. "Leastways," he sniffed, "when I bring my *nee'ka's* sister home to her, 'twill be naught but channel for me."

All the warriors save one shared a laugh. Death was too preoccupied with the horror that was to come to join in.

Kari — Kara — belonged to him. Did it become necessary to offer his life to spare hers, he would do so without hesitation.

And he would await his beloved at the Rah.

To Be Continued...

In

NO WAY OUT: DARI

Made in the USA
Middletown, DE
01 April 2019